THE SYDING ADVENTURES

LIVE WIRES

AND

LOBSTER POTS

WRITTEN BY **5** MARY WEEKS MILLARD

© Day One Publications 2014

First printed 2014

ISBN 978-1-84625-368-3

All Scripture quotations are from the **New International Version** 1984
Copyright © 1973, 1978, 1984

Published by Day One Publications
Ryelands Road, Leominster, HR6 8NZ

TEL 01568 613 740 FAX 01568 611 473

email—sales@dayone.co.uk

UK web site—www.dayone.co.uk

This book is entirely a work of fiction. Some actual place names have
been used, but the names of all people and the villages where they live
are entirely fictitious.

Printed by TJ International

Dedication

To Ethan

May you know God's blessing on you
every day of your life.

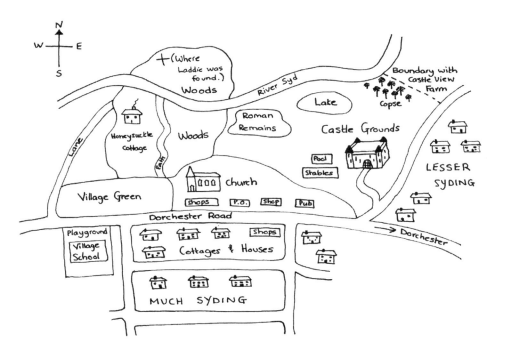

N
W — E
S

+ (Where Laddie was found.)
Woods

River Syd

Boundary with Castle View Farm

Copse

Lake

Honeysuckle Cottage

Woods

Roman Remains

Castle Grounds

Lane

Path

Pool
Stables

LESSER SYDING

Church

Village Green

shops   P.o.   shop   Pub

Dorchester Road

→ Dorchester

Playground
Village School

shops

Cottages & Houses

MUCH SYDING

Map of Much Syding

4

Acknowledgments

I wish to express my grateful thanks to Tirzah Jones, director of Youth Ministries of DayOne and to Chris Jones for her editorial help with this manuscript and to all others involved in the production of the book.

My thanks also to Malcolm, my ever patient and encouraging husband and also to my kind friends who have taken the time to read the manuscript and give their comments.

Chapter One

Paul was feeling cross and fed up. He had been kept in for a detention, and now he had missed the school bus home! It was the first time he had been given a detention since he began at the high school six months ago. He had forgotten to bring his P.E. kit to school, and not only had he missed basketball but also he had to stay after school and tidy up the games cupboard as a punishment. He had overslept that morning and rushed out of the house to catch the bus without thinking about what he needed. Now, he would have to get the normal bus home, and it took ages, winding through lots of villages and stopping so many times! It only ran once an hour, and often it was full too. He had rung his mum to say he would be late so she wouldn't worry. At least he had a mobile!

As Paul had expected, the bus queue was long! He was glad it was a double decker and he could go upstairs and have a seat. To stand all the way home would be the last straw! There were lots of other schoolchildren on the bus, but very few from the high school. Most of them were from the Major Jacob's School, a private school on the other side of the town. Paul didn't like being on the bus with them because they always looked down on the high school pupils, especially the younger ones like him. He looked out of the window. At least the afternoons were lighter now and he could see signs of spring everywhere. Most of the pasture land had sheep grazing with their lambs. That reminded him, he would be late feeding the pigs, and that would make him late doing his homework. What a day it had been!

Paul rang the bell for the bus stop that was near the end of the lane leading to Castle View Farm, where he lived. As he made his way to the stairs, some big boys from Major Jacob's started firstly to hiss and then boo him. Paul found it intimidating, just as the big boys had hoped.

When they saw his face, just a little bit upset, they chanted, 'underclass citizen, underclass citizen'. It made Paul furious. He swore at them, something he had never ever done in his life before. As he started to go downstairs, one big guy gave him a push, making him fall on the stairs, ripping his blazer as he went and then cutting his eyebrow so that blood spattered on his shirt.

What a mess! He managed to get off the bus; the driver looked at him and asked if he was ok.

He mumbled 'yes' and began to walk up the lane. He was shaking all over, angry at himself for swearing. What had made him do that?

As he walked up the lane, dreading what his mum might say about the blazer and the messy shirt, he thought of the rhyme that the primary children used to chant.

"Sticks and stones may break my bones, but words will never hurt me!"

Paul realized that wasn't true. Words hurt very much! He wasn't an 'underclass' and never would be! The words had hurt very much and made him feel inferior. Then he felt ashamed of himself. Why had he sworn? It was out of his mouth before he knew it, and words couldn't be taken back. How he wished they could!

Paul walked through the farm yard and into the kitchen. He knew he had to face his mum. She took one look at him and gasped,

"Whatever has happened to you?"

"I fell down the stairs on the bus," answered Paul, not wanting to tell the whole story, partly because he was afraid his mum might make a complaint to the Major Jacob's School and partly because he was so ashamed at what had come out of his mouth.

"How on earth did you fall?" was her next question, but fortunately she didn't wait for him to answer. "You had better go up and wash your face and change. Let me have your blazer and I'll see if I can mend it for tomorrow, and bring the shirt for me to soak it in cold water."

Paul fled from the kitchen before his mum could ask any more awkward questions. He did as she said, then went out to feed the pigs. It was his job on the farm. All the children had to help in different ways; there was always so much to

8

do. The pigs were actually very clever creatures, and Paul was quite fond of them. Working with them calmed him down a bit before he went to do his homework, and then he put everything ready for the next day. He didn't want any more detentions!

Chapter Two

Paul was the eldest in the Jenkins family. He was almost twelve. His brother Tim was ten and his sister Tessa was nine, and they both attended the nearby primary school in Much Syding. One of the things Paul was finding difficult was that everyone seemed to expect him to become a farmer like his dad and grandad! People said things like, "Well, farming is in his blood!" Paul wasn't at all sure that it was! The trouble was, he had no idea what he did want to do when he grew up. For years, Tim had known he wanted to be a mechanic, and he knew lots about cars and tractors and loved taking things to pieces and then putting them back together again! Tess found school work really hard, but she was brilliant at art, and everyone knew she would be an artist of some sort eventually.

It wasn't that Paul didn't like living on a farm. He loved it and was always happy to help his dad when needed, but he just didn't want to be a farmer. He had seen how hard the life was! They had never been on holiday as a family. The cows needed milking early morning and afternoon each day; in lambing season his dad was up night and day and in bitterly cold weather! Then, there were the crops to sow and harvest. They did employ a farm worker, but he only worked part time. It was also very hard to make the farm pay. His mum and dad often talked about what they might do make more money.

All three children belonged to the Syding Wildlife Society. It was a club which they had formed along with their friends, Theo, Seb and Flick, who lived at Syding Castle in Little Syding village and Tyler, who lived in Honeysuckle Cottage in Much Syding. The family at the castle was hoping one day to have a wildlife sanctuary in their grounds, and so all the children kept wildlife diaries to see what plants and animals lived around them. They had lots of fun together and also adventures! Paul was looking forward to the club meeting on Saturday. He had a really good idea for a fun thing to do. He had told the others to have their 'wellies', fishing nets and buckets ready for action! He hoped it would be a fine day.

In fact, Saturday was one of those bright March days which make you feel that winter has gone and spring is really coming! By the middle of the morning, all the children were free to meet together. They usually met at Syding Castle, because it was about halfway between Tyler's house and the farm and had lots of places where the club could hold its meetings. They began their meeting in the games room, which was in one of the outbuildings. Sebastian, Seb for short, always took charge as the 'chairperson'. He was the oldest, but only just, as Felicity, usually known as Flick, was his twin and only half an hour younger! First of all, he asked everyone about their entries in their nature diaries. They had all seen the same sort of things: the wild violets in the hedges, snowdrops and a few primroses and even celandines. The rabbits were becoming very active in the fields and woods. There had been no 'sightings' of unusual birds, and apart from a nest of rats which Tim had found at the farm, no one had seen any other mammals.

Then it was Paul's turn.

"I have an idea, and that's why I suggested you all had 'wellies' today. I heard something on the radio about crayfish. I know that Theo and Tyler caught some a while back for Tyler's gran. I just thought crayfish were, well, crayfish. Now I have learned that there are two species in England. Our native species is called the white-clawed crayfish and is in danger of becoming extinct because the food supply is being eaten by its American 'big brother' the signal crayfish! Apparently, these were imported to be reared on fish farms and to be sold as food, but they escaped and have now taken over!

"We need to find out which species of crayfish we have in the river. If they are native, they must be protected and it is illegal to take them from the river. If they are American, it is illegal to put them back into the river!"

"How do we know the difference?" asked Theo.

"Well, the signal is a bluish or reddish brown colour, with large, smooth claws, but has a white or pale blue patch by the claw hinge. This is what gives them their name because it's like a small flag which the American train signal men used to wave!" answered Paul.

"How are we going to catch them?" asked Flick, who wasn't too keen on getting wet!

"I understand that they eat almost anything!" Paul explained. "They especially like raw bacon, cheese and sweet corn, but bread will do. I asked mum for some bacon, and she's given me a big hunk. We'll have to cut it up before we go."

"Gran always told me to look for crayfish in clean water and to look under the overhanging trees. There are lots of willows by the river," said Tyler.

"Do we bait a line and hook with the bacon?" Seb asked.

"Yes," answered Paul, "But this is where we all come in and have to work as a team. Crayfish are very easily spooked and can move really, really fast. We have to have one person with a baited line. As soon as the crayfish takes the bait, that person has to pull up the line while their partner scoops the crayfish into the net, then puts it into the bucket of water. If it's a native white claw, then we will put it back, and if not, then Tyler's gran gets a good supper!"

"Who's game to try?" added Paul.

"Wow, it sounds like good fun!" said Tim, and they all agreed.

They soon cut up the bait, and Paul gave a line to Seb, who was to work with Flick and Tess; another to the 'Two T's', as Theo and Tyler were called, and then he and Tim had the last line. They took their nets and buckets and the bait and started walking through the castle estate to the river.

The river ran through the north of the estate. Just a few months earlier, the Ministry for the Environment had changed the river's course to stop flooding, which regularly damaged local buildings and farm land. An artificial lake had been made to drain the excess water, and when all this had been completed, Tyler had come up with the brilliant idea of a wildlife sanctuary. When the new riverbed had been dug out, a Roman site was discovered in the castle grounds, and that was in the process of being excavated, too. It had all been very exciting!

The children reached the river and walked along the bank until they came to the place where the new course had merged again with the original route. They had decided there was more likelihood of finding crayfish where the riverbed had not been disturbed. They reached one spot where they saw several overhanging willow trees. The water looked crystal clear.

"We'll start here!" said Tyler.

"Ok, we'll go a bit further downstream," Seb commented. "How about you going to the other side of the willows?" he suggested to Paul.

It took a few minutes even to get the sticky bacon onto the hooks, and the 'netter' had to be ready to scoop as soon as the crayfish took the bait. It was hilarious! There were several crayfish, and they all seemed hungry, but it was ages before anyone actually scooped one up! It was Tess who made the first catch, and she was very proud of herself. They all peered at it. Without any doubt it was the American invader! At least they now knew what they were looking for!

Eventually, they got the hang of it and caught several crayfish, but they were all 'signals'.

"Guess Gran needed a good supper!" said a rather disappointed Tyler, whose ambition in life was to be a conservationist. He had so hoped to find the native species still in the river.

The bait was almost used up, and they had caught nine good-sized crayfish when Paul decided they should give up the hunt as it was lunchtime.

"I'm just using our last bit of bacon," Theo called out, "Ready, Ty?" Tyler was ready with his fishing net. A crayfish took the bite, and he scooped the animal, almost falling into the river himself. To his delight, when he looked carefully, it was definitely not a 'signal'. No sign of a blue or white flag on the claw hinge. Everyone crowded around to examine it. They were all convinced they had found a native white-clawed crayfish! What an exciting way to end the morning! They carefully set it free in the river.

"That was a fantastic idea, Paul," remarked Flick. "It's been huge fun. We must do it often so that we get rid of all the 'signals' and allow the natives to thrive."

"It reminds me of the red squirrels we saw at Brownsea Island," Tyler said. "I was so excited to see them. If only the American grey squirrels had not been introduced, we would still have them in lots of places in our country!"

"At least our otter population is growing again," commented Theo, "and the American mink invaders seem to be under control!"

They carried their catch carefully through the estate and back to the castle. Theo said he would help Tyler carry them down to his gran. Tyler belonged to a Romany gypsy family, and his gran still lived in her traditional painted wagon or 'vardo'. She would be so excited about the crayfish!

Chapter Three

The 'Two T's' carried the crayfish in two buckets balanced on the handlebars of Tyler's bike all the way to Much Syding, then through the woods to Honeysuckle Cottage. His gran was sitting on the little steps to her vardo, watching Tyler's almost-three-year-old sister playing with her kitten. She looked up when she saw the boys.

"What have you there?" she asked, pointing to the buckets.

"A surprise for your tea!" said Tyler. "We've been catching crayfish in the river!"

"We have nine for you," Theo added. "We know you like them!"

"That's wonderful! Thank you so much," she answered, her wrinkly old face lighting up with happiness.

"I shall make a fire and boil them. They are nicest cooked over an open fire. The smell of the wood gets into them. I must find some herbs and make a sauce for them. What a lovely supper I will have!"

Sunshine came over to look at the creatures in the buckets. She didn't like the look of their claws and picked up her kitten and ran into the house.

The boys began to collect some wood for Gran's fire. Nobody really knew how old Gran was; she wasn't even sure herself. When she was a child, many Romany people

17

weren't registered, so they didn't have birth certificates. As a child, Gran had grown up travelling from one place to another all through the year. She had never been to school so was unable to read or write. Even so, she was very wise and knew many things about the countryside. She was good with a knife too and could carve from wood. As a young woman she had made clothes pegs to sell from door to door. Sometimes, when her parents had stayed on a farm to help with harvesting potatoes or peas, she and her brothers and sisters would work in the fields. Life was always very hard but a lot of fun, too. As a teenager, Gran had learned the trade of most Romany women, to tell fortunes. Then she travelled from fair to fair through the summertime to make enough money to live through the winter. She hadn't understood that it was wrong to tell fortunes. It was many, many years later, after her daughter, Tyler's mother, had become a Christian, that she had also learned about Jesus and also that telling fortunes was something forbidden by God. He alone knows the secrets of the heart and the future.

When she was only sixteen years old, a husband had been chosen for her. In those days there was no 'dating' between boys and girls. Her parents chose a boy from a good Romany family. Weddings are always times of great partying for the gypsies, and her wedding had been no exception! Her parents had chosen a kind young man, and they had been happy together. He, like most Romany men, had been a skilled boxer, as well as good at doing many odd jobs. He had smoked from a very young age and eventually developed cancer in his lungs. The treatment had not been so good then, and he had died within a few months, leaving Gran to bring up six children on her own. Her parents and other gypsy relatives always travelled with her, so she had some help and support, but very little money.

It had been a hard life in many ways, but Gran had saved enough to buy a little house for her only daughter so that one day she could settle down. That little house was Honeysuckle Cottage. Several months ago, Gran had joined the family, living in her vardo just behind the cottage. She preferred it that way, but now that spring was coming, Gran had a great urge to take to the road again.

Only that morning she had found her daughter, Betty, moving all the furniture around in the cottage. She knew that Betty did that to stifle the urge to go travelling. It was hard for those who had been born and brought up as travellers to settle down, especially in the spring. The great outdoors and open road called them. She had made some tea, so she called her daughter over to chat to her.

Gran felt that she needed to make one last journey so that once again she could to meet up with her relatives and friends.

"The urge is very strong, Betty. I have prayed and prayed and asked God if I should travel again. I feel that many of my own generation of Romanies have never heard about Jesus. I want to tell them to give up their fortune telling and trust in Jesus while they can. He has made such a difference in my life. I used to have so many fears, but now I have so many joys. I am very old, maybe eighty or more years. I was a grown girl when the war came. You are my only daughter and my youngest child. Do you understand that I need to make this journey?"

Tyler's mum had been taken aback by her mother's suggestion. She hadn't expected Gran ever to take to the road again, but she understood because inside she too felt the same urge to travel once more.

At lunch time she talked to her husband, Bill. He came up with a suggestion.

"Why don't you and Sunshine go with Gran? That way you can take care of her and keep her company. Sunshine can meet her family and learn what it is like to take to the road before she starts at pre-school.

"If Gran feels God wants her to share her faith with her family, then you can support her and pray for her. It will not be easy."

"But what about Tyler?" asked Betty.

"Tyler and I will manage fine! He always goes to Theo's after school, and if there is ever a problem, then I can leave work early or he can come and help me in the woods," answered Bill.

Tyler's father was a woodsman for the Forestry Commission, looking after the extensive woods at Much Syding and a few other nearby places.

So once Tyler's parents had prayed together, Betty went over to put the suggestion to Gran. Gran was delighted! She wanted to start making plans to move off at once, but Betty said she needed to fill the freezer for her boys first.

All this had happened while Tyler was out catching crayfish! When they told him that evening, he was surprised at first and then disappointed that he wasn't going too! He would miss his mum, sister and gran very much, but he knew that he and his dad would have great times together, and he promised to help his dad all he could. Even he understood this great need to travel. He was proud of his Romany heritage.

Chapter Four

Theo came bursting in through the door, having pedalled as fast as he could from Tyler's house.

"Mum, guess what?" he said excitedly.

"How can I guess?" laughed his mum. "You'd better spill the beans. I can see you are bursting with news!"

"Gran wants to go off travelling again! She says it's the 'call of the road' in spring! 'Auntie' Betty doesn't want her to go alone, so she and Sunshine are going too. They could be gone for weeks!"

Theo's mum sat down, looking quite shaken at this news. Betty was not only her best friend, but she also was always willing to come and help run the B and B when things got busy.

"They just decided at lunchtime today," Theo remarked. "Tyler was a bit shocked, but he and his dad will have lots of fun together. His dad said they had prayed about it and felt it was right to support Gran. She wants to make one last trip to see all her Romany relatives and tell them about Jesus. She doesn't know how old she is but thinks she's so old she may not get another chance."

"When are they going?" asked Theo's mum. "We must get Flick to give Sparks an extra special grooming."

Sparks was the pony which pulled Gran's vardo. He was
a good, strong and reliable pony. Since Gran had 'retired'
from the travelling way of life, Sparks had been stabled in
the castle's empty stable block and Flick, who adored horses,
had looked after him. All the children rode him from time to
time, but Flick took him out most days. She would miss him.

With a heavy heart, Theo's mum got on with her work. A
young couple was arriving to stay for two nights. They were
due any time, and she wanted to offer them some tea after
their long journey. She tried to do little extras like this to
make people feel at home. A plate of cupcakes was already
on the kitchen table, and she gently tapped Theo's hand as
he reached out for one.

"Not yet, young man!" she said. "You wait until your
teatime. Go and see to your chickens first."

The children at the castle all had jobs to do to help their
mum. A couple of years ago, their father had left home
and gone to Australia with a young woman. Now they were
married and had a baby daughter, Lucy Jane. The castle
children had never seen their half-sister, but the previous
December they had seen their dad and he had shown them a
photo.

Before their dad had left, they had been very well-off and
had had everything they wanted, attending expensive private
schools and having holidays abroad every year. It had been
a terrible shock when he had gone and their mother had

had to cope with a million-pound mortgage. At first he had sent a little maintenance money for the children, but this soon fizzled out. They left their private schools and started at the local ones. It had been hard at first to adapt and make friends, but it was at Much Syding Primary School that Theo had met Tyler. Through their friendship, the two families had become good friends and not only that, Theo had become a Christian, followed by his mother and older sister, Penny. Seb and Flick were quite interested and usually joined Theo at the Live Wires group at Much Syding Church on Sunday mornings and occasionally at the Faith is Fun (FIF's) group at school. They had not made up their minds yet about Christianity.

At first, the family thought they would have to sell their beloved castle home. Then they decided to all pull together and help their mum run a bed and breakfast business. They all had jobs to do, and one of Theo's was to look after the two ducks and ten hens. He loved them! He fed them each day, unlocked them to roam free before he went to school and made sure they were safely in the coop at night. Best of all, he liked hunting for the eggs!

Penelope, the eldest in the family, had just turned sixteen. She was an amazing musician and had won a scholarship to a music academy in Manchester. Her dream was to become a concert pianist, and all the family were sure she would achieve it. Since she had gone away to boarding school,

Tyler's mum, Betty, came to help out at the castle when she was needed. They had many interesting people come to stay as guests. Theo wondered what the young couple, who were arriving that evening, would be like.

He didn't have to wonder for long as a car drew up outside the front door and a young couple got out. The young lady rang the bell while the man took the cases out of the car. His mother answered, and they were shown inside. Theo went through the kitchen door and put the eggs by the sink, ready for washing.

After his mother had shown the couple to their room, she came down to make them some tea.

"They seem a very nice couple," his mum remarked. "Mr and Mrs Porter. I'm glad the sun is shining for them. I'm taking the tea into the lounge. Can you run and switch the fire on for them, Theo?"

Theo went to do as he was asked and glimpsed the couple coming down the main staircase.

"I'm Theo," he introduced himself. "I've just put the fire on in the lounge for you. Mum is bringing your tea and some scrumptious cupcakes!"

"Hello, Theo," the young lady smiled at him. He thought she looked very friendly. "I'm Amy and this is Dan, my husband. Thank you for looking after us. What a fantastic home you have here!"

"We love it," said Theo proudly. "If you like, I can give you a conducted tour after you have had your tea. I have the turret as my bedroom, but there are a hundred steps to reach it! The view is wonderful. I can see for miles around, even as far as my friends' house at Castle View Farm!"

"We'd really like a tour, wouldn't we darling?" replied Dan. "Can you spare the time to take us round?"

"Of course I can. Saturdays are nice, no homework," answered Theo. "But later I do have to swim. We have our own pool, and I am in the school swimming squad. I'm practising butterfly stroke for the inter-schools' gala. Nobody else wanted to do butterfly, so I thought I'd give it a try as I can practice every day."

"Hey! Can we join you in the pool, or is it only for family?" asked Amy. "I didn't know there was a pool here. I used to swim for Wales when I was at school and also swam butterfly. I might be able to give you a few tips!"

"Would you really?" Theo was excited now. "This gala is very important to me. Mum never minds guests using the pool so long as they understand that the family might be swimming, too. The twins are going to the cinema in Dorchester this evening, so they won't want to swim. That's my older brother Seb and sister, Flick. They're thirteen."

Theo's mum came in with the tea and cakes. "Let Mr and Mrs Porter have their tea in peace," she told Theo. They laughed. "Please call us Amy and Dan, we'd much rather, and Theo has kindly offered to show us round the castle and then allow us to swim with him in the pool, if that's ok with you," answered Dan.

The tour of the castle took ages because Dan and Amy were really interested in everything, including the wildlife lake and wildflower meadow which had been planted, the archaeological excavations and even the old chapel which had recently been discovered in the cellars. Theo proudly told them all about the finding of a Tyndale New Testament, which was at Dorchester Museum at present and how they wanted to turn the old chapel back into a 'prayer space' for the castle. This is when he learned that they were Christians working in Burundi, helping very poor people who had returned to their own country after many years away as refugees. Theo wasn't at all sure where Burundi was, except that it was somewhere in Africa.

He really was interested, though, and said he would love to hear more about their lives if they had time to share later on. Usually his mum had a very strict rule about not asking guests lots of questions, but this couple seemed different. They really wanted to be friends.

They all met up at the swimming pool, which once used to be a magnificent greenhouse, but Theo's father had had it converted to a pool. Normally all through the winter and early spring it wasn't used because it cost so much to heat, but this year, Theo's mum had tried to keep it going so that he could get lots of practice. Theo was a bit shy knowing he was swimming with somebody who had represented Wales, but after a few minutes he forgot about that and just enjoyed the sheer pleasure of moving through the water. Amy was really encouraging. She helped him get a slightly better stroke and gave him some very helpful tips. She laughed when she heard that he really loved freestyle but that no one else was prepared to have a go at butterfly, so he had volunteered.

"Don't worry. You've got a really good stroke. You'll probably 'knock the socks off' everyone else! Just keep practising and try to remember the things I've shown you," she said.

Amy and Dan had booked a table at a restaurant in Dorchester, so they had to go and get ready, and it was almost suppertime for the family.

"I hope I see you at breakfast tomorrow," said Theo. "Mum lets us help serve our guests. Then I go to Live Wires group at the Much Syding Church."

"I'm sure we will see you, and if you'll let us, we would like to go to church too," answered Dan.

Theo was so pleased. He went to supper full of the news of his new friends. His mum sounded very interested and hoped she would be able to get to church too and maybe ask her guests about Burundi.

Chapter Five

C hurch began at ten-thirty, and it was always a rush
for the Jenkins family to get there. Sometimes Dad
just couldn't make it if the ewes were still lambing or a cow
calving. Paul rushed around looking after the pigs, and then
he had to shower and change. He couldn't very well turn
up smelling like a pigsty! This Sunday he wished he could
find some excuse and stay at home, but he couldn't think of
anything which his mum would believe. He usually really
enjoyed 'Live Wires', but ever since he had sworn in the bus,
he had felt guilty and bad about himself.

"Hurry up, Paul," called his mum. She was already starting
up the car, and Tim and Tess were sitting in the back seats.
He grabbed his Bible from the shelf and squeezed in beside
his brother.

"Move over," he said gruffly, pushing Tim quite hard.

"What's ruffled your feathers this morning?" asked his dad
as he climbed into the front passenger seat.

Tessa giggled at that phrase, and that made Paul even
madder. In his head he swore again, but he didn't dare say
such a thing out loud in front of his family. What was the
matter with him? He didn't really want to behave so badly,
but something inside of him seemed to be pushing him.

They all went into the church. It was peaceful and beautiful, and normally Paul loved to sit and hear the organ playing and enjoy the ten minutes or so of the service before they went out for their group. Today, he felt as if everyone could see inside him and knew what a horrid boy he was! He noticed the castle family arriving and with them a young couple. He wondered who they were. Theo, Seb and Flick hadn't said yesterday that they had visitors coming to stay. They looked nice, he thought. Then Tyler and his family sat in the row opposite him. Gran looked very chirpy and so did Tyler's mum. Maybe it was the crayfish! They had really had fun catching them! Paul was pleased that he had thought of the idea. It was the only good thing about the weekend, he thought grumpily.

The children who were between the ages of seven and fourteen went to the 'Live Wires' group. In the group they split again into those at primary school and those at senior. The senior group watched a DVD that was the story of some of the wars which had occurred in the last half-century between different people groups in various countries. It was terrible to see fighting between people who all spoke the same language and belonged in the same country but maybe had a different religion or belonged to a different class of society. They discussed together how such hate might start and grow in a community.

The leader then asked the children to look in their Bibles at what Jesus had to say in Matthew's gospel in the passage called 'The Sermon on the Mount' in chapters five to the beginning of seven. They looked at several verses about forgiveness for those who misuse and hate you and about not judging other people and loving your enemies. It was all very challenging, and the children discussed instances when they had been hurt and needed to forgive.

Paul listened but didn't say much. He just felt so bad about his reaction when he was ridiculed on the bus. He knew in his heart of hearts that he should forgive, but something kept making him stubborn.

Just before the group ended, the leader told the children about a plan he was making.

"I thought it would be really good if we had a weekend away during the Easter holidays. If you are interested, can you ask your parents to ring me so that I can go ahead and book it up?"

Everyone looked very interested at this proposal. It would be such fun! Even Paul cheered up at the prospect. He was sure his parents would let him go if he asked them. Theo was very enthusiastic at first but then he realised that his mum might need him if she had lots of visitors, and his face fell.

"What's wrong, Theo?" the leader enquired as the group was dispersing. "You don't look very happy!"

"Well," he replied, "I would love to go on the weekend trip, but I realised that Mum might need me. You see, Tyler's mum usually helps out with visitors, especially at busy times like the Easter holidays, but now she's going off travelling in the vardo with his gran and may be away for weeks."

The Live Wires leader thought for a moment, then had an idea.

"Maybe your mother would like to put an advert in the church newsletter to see if someone else could help while Tyler's mum is away? Why don't you suggest it?"

"That is a good idea! I'll certainly tell her about that. I'm still not sure that all three of us could be away for the whole weekend, though," Theo replied, "but I will tell her about it."

The three families all went home quite excited about the possibility of going away for a weekend with the Live Wires in the Easter holidays. However, none of the children had time to talk about it with their parents because each of them had very busy afternoons.

Tyler's gran wanted to start her trip at once! In true gypsy fashion, she and Betty were able to pack up and begin travelling very quickly. Tyler was sent over to the castle to fetch Sparks the pony. Flick had beautifully groomed him, and it almost seemed as if he understood that he was going to travel again—his eyes were bright and he flicked his tail in excitement! Tyler rode him back to Honeysuckle Cottage where his dad hitched him up in the shafts of the vardo.

Betty, his mum, was brimming over with happiness. and Sunshine was settling her little kitten in its basket inside the van, only to find she wasn't allowed to take her on the journey! That was quite a blow, but with all the excitement she soon got over it. Even Tyler and his dad felt the excitement in the air, although they knew they would miss their 'girls' while they were away. At least these days they all had mobiles and could keep in touch!

Once they had gone, Tyler and his dad went into their cottage. It seemed very quiet inside, and outside there was a huge empty space where the vardo had been parked. However, Bill, Tyler's dad, had already thought of something which would keep both of them busy while the 'girls' were away. He called Tyler to come to the kitchen table and brought out a roll of paper on which he had drawn some plans.

"I thought," he said to Tyler, "that while everyone is gone, we could build a log cabin in the yard. It would make a club house for your 'Wildlife Society', be a play house for Sunshine when she is older and even be a place where your cousins could stay when they visit. If it goes well and we still have time, we might be able to make a treehouse as well in the large sycamore tree in the garden. What do you think?"

"Oh, dad!" answered Tyler, "That is such a brilliant idea! In a couple of weeks, the clocks change and we can work in the evenings!"

"Yes, that's fine, so long as the homework is all done properly. I would like you to go home from school with Theo as usual, and I'll collect you when I finish work. Don't forget we have to cook for ourselves and do the washing up, plus other things Mum always does," said his dad, "Also, I've not mentioned this to Mum or Gran, so keep it a secret—a surprise for them to come home to! I'll go to the wood merchant tomorrow and order what we need, and we'll start as soon as it arrives. Meanwhile, let's see what we can cook for our supper. I may teach you to cook outside, Romany fashion."

Somehow, with the thought of building a log cabin, Tyler felt quite excited and decided that he and his dad, just the two of them, would have a lot of fun together. Just before bedtime, he remembered to ask his father about the proposed weekend away with the Live Wires. His dad thought it would be a great chance for him to go away with his friends and promised to phone the leader and find out the details.

Paul didn't say anything to his parents about the weekend when they drove home from church because it was only for the senior group of Live Wires, and he didn't want to upset Tim and Tessa by talking about it. He thought he would talk to his father when they were sorting out the pigs that evening. However, when they arrived home, they found there was a visitor on the doorstep. It was Jack, their father's elderly uncle. Great-uncle Jack lived in a small cottage on the edge of Chesil beach in Portland. He was a bachelor who had been a fisherman all of his life and was now well into his eighties. No one in the family was exactly sure how old he was because he couldn't remember himself. If the children asked him, he would smile at them and say, "As old as my tongue and a little older than my teeth!" and they would laugh at that but be no wiser as to his real age. When he was young, he must have been a strong and handsome man, for even in his old age he was quite big, had a shock of white hair and a crinkly, weather-beaten face. All the children adored him. He was full of stories about his long life, especially about fishing on the Fleet lagoon and about Chesil beach. He had walked all the way to visit them. That was the sort of old man he was, still strong enough to walk miles, and he preferred to do that to catching an 'omnibus', as he still called a bus.

Everyone was delighted to see Great-uncle Jack, and an extra place was soon laid at the table. Sunday dinner was still a special occasion for the Castle View farm family. Most of the food came from their own farm, and their mum was renowned as the best cook in the neighbourhood. There was always plenty for them all with enough to spare, and Mum loved having unexpected guests.

After dinner Paul stayed at the table sitting with the grown-ups, hoping Uncle Jack would tell one of his stories. Tim and Tess had gone off to play hide and seek together, a favourite treat at the weekend, before they went out with their nature diaries to see what they could find. Uncle Jack cleared his throat and began to explain his real reason for visiting today.

"It came to me t'other day," he began in his broad Dorset dialect, "that one of these 'ere days I shall have to give up me fishing. When your'n lad twere knee-high to a grass'opper, I did make a promise to 'ee. I promised I'd take 'im out fishing in me boats and we'd catch lobsters! Well, I think 'tis about time we did that. 'Ow about next Saturday, me lad?" he asked, turning to Paul.

Paul turned bright pink with excitement. "I'd so love that, Uncle Jack. That is," he said, looking at his parents, "if it's ok with Mum and Dad."

His parents nodded in agreement, and so they made arrangements to take Paul the following Saturday to his great-uncle's cottage as soon as the early morning milking was finished. Before he left the grown-ups to chat together, Paul decided maybe it was the right time to ask about the Live Wires weekend trip. He explained that it was just for the senior group and that he would love to go. Once again, his parents agreed it was ok and promised to phone the leader for more details. Paul was so happy as he went outside to see his pigs. Two treats to look forward to! Yet, inside a little niggly thought kept coming to him that he didn't deserve them.

Chapter Six

Amy and Dan had been pleased to go to the village church with the family from the castle. Although they had planned to have a quiet weekend away in the country and had chosen Little Syding Castle because it looked quaint and romantic, they really liked meeting new people and had loved being taken on a tour of the castle and grounds by Theo. They always got excited when they made friends with other Christians; it really was like being in one big family!

After the service, they had planned to go into Dorchester with a picnic, but then Sally, the children's mother, invited them to have lunch with the family if they would like to do so.

"Thank you so much," answered Dan. "We would love to. Then afterwards we can have a walk in the woods and by the river."

Sally drove home with the twins, while Theo walked back with his new friends.

"Can you tell me about Burundi?" he asked them. "I know it is in Africa, but that is all."

Amy laughed. "I was just the same when I first heard someone talk about the terrible civil war that lasted thirteen years and the awful conditions many people have to live in. I had to get out a map and find out where Burundi was.

Have you got an atlas? If you have, I'll show you exactly where it is when we get back to your home. It is a small country, almost in the middle of Africa. It's easy to find as it has a border along Lake Tanganyika. Sitting on top of it is Rwanda, another small country, and it shares some of its history and culture. Their languages are very similar, and both have endured terrible civil wars in recent years. Many people have heard of the genocide in Rwanda because it was so sudden and so many people were killed, but it has been equally bad in Burundi, though spread out over more years."

"I had just finished my training as a nurse and then as a midwife and wanted to help in a developing country before I settled down to a long-term job in Wales," explained Amy. "I was thinking about this and started to ask God what His plan for my life might be when a businessman came to speak at our church. He had been trying to start some business developments in Burundi because the people are so poor and there is so little work available. In fact, Burundi is the poorest nation in the world! This guy showed a powerpoint presentation so that we could see how needy the people are. When I saw mothers with tiny babies trying to make a sort of shelter just on the sides of the dirt roads, I was shocked! I went home and cried and told the Lord that I would go and help if I could."

Amy took a deep breath and continued, "My parents were quite worried when I told them that I wanted to go to

Burundi to work. Anyway, to cut a long story short, I found a job working with a charity that helps refugees. I have been helping with mainly widows and orphans. I quickly fell in love with the country."

"And that's not all she fell in love with!" added Dan. "I was working out there with a different charity that helps to rebuild houses, schools and hospitals after they have been destroyed by natural disasters or war, and when we met … we fell in love and got married last year."

"That's an amazing story!" said Theo. "You must tell my mum, Seb and Flick too!"

They had just entered the castle grounds when Dan commented on the lions which stood on pillars on either side of the entrance to the castle.

"I love them," Theo told him. "They remind me of the story in the Bible of Daniel in the lions' den. It was the first Bible story I ever read, and that was last summer. I loved it so much and then began to read more and more because I was helping my friend Tyler to read and he wanted to be able to read the Bible to his mum and dad. You see, they are Romany gypsies and had never been to school properly and so could not read. When they became Christians, they had a problem because they could not read the Bible."

"That's a good story too!" Dan remarked.

"And it has a really cool ending," continued Theo. "I'll tell you about it later on."

After dinner Amy and Dan went off to have a walk. It was quite a bright day and just right for walking. It gave Theo, Seb and Flick time to ask their mum about the Live Wires weekend. When she heard about it, she sighed.

"I'd so love you all to go. Penny will be home for the holidays, and I'm sure she will help me with the guests. I already have a lot of bookings for the Easter period. I don't want her to be working all the time though, for she has her practice to do and also revision for her exams. Can you give me a few days to think about it?"

"Of course, Mum," said Seb, speaking for them all. Then Theo piped up:

"Actually, the leader had a good idea. When I told him that we might not be able to go because you needed help and Auntie Betty has gone travelling, he said, 'Why don't you put an advert in the church newsletter asking for some temporary help?'"

Sally smiled. "Why not? I certainly hadn't thought of that! I'll write out a notice and take it to the church office tomorrow. If someone replies who is suitable, then there is no reason why you shouldn't all go away for that weekend. I'll ring your leader in any case, so that I have all the details."

The twins and Theo were delighted. It looked as if they would be able to go! Then they decided to go out for a bike ride for the rest of the afternoon. When they returned, Amy and Dan had come back and said they would like to swim again. Theo joined them as he wanted to practice the tips which Amy had given him about the butterfly stroke.

After supper, Theo told his mum and the twins about the work which Amy and Dan were doing in Burundi.

"I wonder if Live Wires could do some fundraising to help the refugees," Flick suggested. "It could be good fun, and we'd be helping other people."

"Why don't you ask Amy and Dan at breakfast tomorrow?" suggested their mum. "They asked for it early because they want to get on their way, back to Wales. You can help me serve the breakfasts so that you will have the opportunity to ask them then. It sounds a good idea to me."

The next morning, all three children were up in good time to help with breakfasts before catching the school bus. Flick then told Amy and Dan about her idea that they could fundraise to help the refugees in Burundi. Amy and Dan were thrilled and promised to write and give them all the information they needed.

"Every little helps. Even one pound buys much more in Burundi than it does here. It sounds such a wonderful idea, and we would be so grateful for any help!"

"We'll have a meeting and come up with some ideas," said Seb, who really liked organizing things.

The children went on to school and even on the bus were thinking of things they could do to raise money. Meanwhile,

Amy and Dan packed their belongings and went to say goodbye to Sally.

"We've loved staying here with you and your lovely family!" Amy said. "We will send the details we've promised. If we can, we would like to come for another night or so before we go back to Africa."

"Please come again! Next time you will be our guests. It will be my part of the 'fundraising' to treat you!" Sally added.

Chapter Seven

*P*aul was so looking forward to his outing with Great-uncle Jack the following weekend. Through the week he worked hard at school and also at his homework. He tried to push the incident on the bus out of his mind. He certainly made sure that he was out of school in time to catch the special bus home with the 'Two T's'. Each evening he watched the TV weather forecast, hoping and praying that it would stay calm enough for the trip. On Friday evening, Paul put his 'wellies' and old warm anorak ready to wear. His mum made a mountain of sandwiches for both him and his uncle, and he set the alarm for five a.m.

When the alarm rang, he woke up and tried to be as quiet as he could getting ready for the adventure. Outside he could hear the milking machines at work, so he grabbed some cereal and toast while he waited for his dad to finish. The farmhand was washing down the byre and sending the cows back to the pasture, and his dad came in to have a quick breakfast and then drive Paul to Portland. The roads were very quiet at that time of the day, and they only took about three-quarters of an hour to get to Chiswell, the village where Great-uncle Jack lived. His uncle's cottage was right by the beach, the legendary Chesil beach which stretches from Portland all the way around the coast to Lyme

Regis. The cottage had been built with a channel flowing through it from the back door through the hall to the front door. In the old days when Uncle Jack had been a boy, there had been no flood defences, so when a storm came, the sea washed right over Chesil beach, through the house and out the other side!

Uncle insisted that they all have a cup of tea and another round of toast and marmalade. This amazing old man even made his own marmalade, and it was delicious. Then Paul's dad said he must get back to the farm. He checked that Paul had his mobile and asked him to phone when it was time to come home. Uncle did have a landline in the house but almost nothing else which belonged to the twenty-first century.

Great-uncle Jack took Paul into the tiny kitchen.

"We need to cut up the bait first," he explained. "I've some mackerel which were caught yest'day. It be a bit messy, but we'll cut it into lumps, which we'll tie into the lobster pots. When 'tis done, we'll go over shore and ready the pots. I'm right glad you've come, lad, 'cos March 15th is end of the season for fishing lobsters. It don't start again 'til October 15th, and I might not be 'round then!"

"What do you mean, Uncle Jack, you might not be around? Are you planning on going somewhere?" asked Paul, a bit puzzled because Uncle Jack had not left Portland ever in his life.

44

Uncle Jack laughed, his old, weather-beaten face crinkling up.

"Well, me laddie," he said, "I'm a good age. One of these days the good Lord will come for us. I want to keep me promise to thee afore that 'appens."

When the bait was ready, they took the pail out of the back door and climbed over the high ridge of pebbles and down to the shore where the small rowing boat was pulled up. Uncle Jack handed Paul a life jacket and showed him how to put it on. Then Paul helped Uncle Jack haul the boat down to the sea; they climbed in and his uncle began to row.

"One day, I'll take 'ee to the Fleet and teach 'ee to row. The sea's too dangerous," he told Paul. The Fleet is an inland lagoon which nestles behind Chesil beach for some miles and is protected from the strong currents which swirl around Portland.

Paul's uncle rowed them across the small bay to where his fishing boat, the *Lady Lucy*, was anchored.

"Lucy twere me ma's name," Uncle Jack explained, "so I called the boat after her. Climb aboard, lad, and then I'll tie the dinghy behind."

Paul did as he was told. He held tight to the sides as it swayed so much, and he didn't want to fall into the sea. It might not be very deep and he could swim well, but in March it would be very cold. The boat was much bigger than the rowing boat, but it was not a modern boat, even though Uncle had kept it well maintained. On the deck there were several lobster pots all strung together by a rope, and each one had a pink buoy near it. The buoy was numbered, and Paul's uncle explained that it was his license number. Other fishermen and also the authorities would know that the pots belonged to him. Uncle Jack showed Paul how to put the bait into the pots and they did this together, Uncle teaching him a sea shanty as they did it. Paul was interested in the pots, and his uncle told him how as a young man he had woven the pots from willow and then made them sea worthy by coating them with tar. These days, he went on to tell him, they were made from modern materials, but they all had the same requirement. The trap's hole must be the right size so that any small lobsters can swim out and escape and only the large ones are caught.

Paul was surprised how quickly the time went. Before they went out to the fishing area to collect the pots which had been out all night and hopefully contained some lobsters, Uncle Jack suggested they eat some of the sandwiches Paul's mother had made for them. Paul was starving. The sea air certainly gave him an appetite. Then his uncle started the engine and showed Paul how to steer the boat, and off they went to the lobster grounds. The pink buoys guided them to the pots. Paul was so excited as they hauled them up and found lobsters in them. Very deftly, his uncle released the lobsters into a deep tank on board. They progressed around the island, picking up the pots and emptying them. It then was time to set out the newly-baited pots. By this time they had sailed around the 'Bill', where the lighthouse stood brightly painted in red and white. Once or twice Uncle Jack looked at the sky, which seemed to be gathering clouds.

"We'll start to put these pots down now, lad," he said to Paul and showed him how they were gently placed in the water with each buoy marking the spot. Paul hadn't noticed the weather changing—he was so absorbed with helping Uncle Jack—but the old seafarer looked a little worried. In the springtime, the tides could be fierce and storms suddenly brew up. It looked as if this was what was happening now.

"See them white hosses," Uncle Jack pointed out to sea at the angry white waves. "'Tis the Portland races. We'em best head near the shore, lad, but not too near them rocks."

He took the wheel and began to steer against the wind and waves, closer to the rocky shore. Now Paul could see his uncle's face was creased with worry. Once Paul began to look at the waves, he began to feel a bit sick. He had no idea the sea could change so quickly but was sure he would be alright. His uncle had fished these waters for over half a century.

Chapter Eight

The *Lady Lucy* was being battered by the storm. The waves were incredibly high and swept over the deck.

"We best 'bandon her," shouted Uncle Jack against the noise of the storm. "I'll admit it, I'm afeared for us." Then he reached into the cabin and brought out a distress flare and lit it.

"Coastguards'll see it and alert the lifeboat; never fear, lad," he said, but Paul was afraid, very afraid. He reached in his pocket and tried to phone his dad, but there was no signal. Suddenly a huge wave washed over the boat, and he lost his balance and the phone.

Paul wondered what would happen to them. Would they both drown? Uncle Jack might be sure the good Lord would come for him, but Paul was much less sure for himself. Suddenly in his misery, he called out to Jesus to help them.

"I don't want to drown or die," he cried. "Forgive me and save us!"

Old as he was, Uncle Jack was incredibly fit and strong. Against the waves, he managed to bring the dinghy close enough and almost threw Paul into it and then jumped down. The poor little rowing boat rocked and was pretty full of water. Paul tried to bail it out as best he could while Uncle Jack somehow, miraculously, rowed towards the shore.

Then they were sucked inwards by the undertow and landed up being drawn into a cave. At least it seemed their lives were safe, for now!

The rowing boat was resting on sand at the entrance to the cave. Great-uncle Jack jumped out, and Paul followed him. Together they dragged the boat out of the shallow water and well into the cave. It was hard to tell whether the tide was still coming in or had turned. The cave seemed to go back into the land a long way, and it was dark! However, for the moment, they were just glad to be alive and in a safe place! Uncle Jack found a rock and sat on it. Paul could see how old and tired he looked, yet his amazing strength had saved them. How had he managed to row against the waves? Surely God must have given him superhuman power! Thinking about God made Paul realise how his prayer had been answered. He had cried out in the boat, feeling sure they would both drown, yet God had heard and answered. Paul had also cried out to God for forgiveness, for he knew his thoughts, words and actions through the past week or so had been wrong, and he had been feeling so guilty. Now he realised too that God had answered that prayer also, for he no longer felt the heaviness that his guilt had been giving him. Somehow he felt light and happy, in spite of being very wet, cold and still far from home.

Paul turned to Uncle Jack and thanked him for saving him. Then he told his great-uncle that in the storm he had cried out to God for his help.

"Me too, laddie," said Uncle Jack. "Me too. Only God could have helped me to row against the tide in them waves, only God!"

"Then I think we should say 'thank you', don't you?" Paul asked him. His uncle nodded, and Paul talked to God for them both.

"Father God, we want to say thank you to you for saving our lives today. Please help us to be found quickly, and don't let our family get worried. Amen," he said.

"Amen to that," Uncle Jack added.

They were both very wet, and Paul could see that Uncle Jack was shivering because of the cold. He knew that old people could die from being too cold—hypothermia, he remembered it was called. He thought that he must get his uncle up and moving.

"I think we should explore this cave a bit, Uncle," he said. "We need to move to keep warm."

"You be right, me laddie," replied Uncle Jack, and Paul helped him to his feet. It was hard for the old man to move; it seemed his joints had seized up. Their clothes were heavy and dripped with sea water. They took off their life jackets and laid them on the big rock where Uncle had sat, and that made it a little easier to walk. Paul made his uncle walk as fast as he could manage without getting out of breath, and they walked further into the cave. Gradually, their eyes became accustomed to the dark, and Paul was able to make out that other people had used this cave too. On one side there was a ledge, probably big enough for a man to lie down, and to his huge delight, Paul found some rope, sacks and an old blanket.

"Look, Uncle!" he exclaimed. "See what I've found! Why don't you take off your wet sweater and wrap yourself in the blanket. It might make your teeth stop chattering."

He helped the old man out of his wet clothes and wrapped him in the blanket. Uncle Jack was too tired and cold to argue.

"What about you, laddie? How are you going to get warm?" Uncle asked Paul.

"I'm going to run," answered Paul. "But while I run up the cave, you must keep moving. Just keep walking around. I'm sure help will soon come!"

Paul began to jog further into the cave. He didn't feel very brave, but he thought he should see if there was a way out. Maybe smugglers had used it in years past and made a tunnel out of it, like the tunnel which the 'Two T's' had found in another part of Portland last term. The cave became very dark and narrow, and the track seemed to have a dead end. Paul was disappointed. Right at the end there was another ledge, and Paul saw there was a tarpaulin covering something. He pulled it off and saw a case. It was a modern case, which he then proceeded to try and open but without any luck as it was locked. He wondered who had hidden it and what could be inside it. Anyway, he decided that he would borrow the tarpaulin for now; it would be something else to keep Uncle Jack warm. He tried to run back down the cave carrying it, but it was heavy and he kept tripping on it, so he ended up walking. At least the sea didn't get up that far in the cave, because the rock floor was quite dry. He wished he had a torch, for he was sure there would be bats clinging on to the walls and roof, and that would have been worth noting in his nature diary.

Eventually, Paul dragged the tarpaulin down to his uncle. This time he suggested they go back to the mouth of the cave, and he let Uncle Jack sit on the rock and did his best to wrap him in the tarpaulin. At least the old man had stopped shivering now.

Paul didn't have much idea of the time, but it seemed a long time since the flare had been fired. He decided to jog and run on the spot at the entrance to the cave. If the lifeboat came anywhere near, maybe they would spot him. Underneath his anorak he wore an old red sweater. He decided to take it off and wave it like a flag. Then he asked his uncle to sing the sea shanty he had taught him earlier. He thought it would keep his spirits up, and he didn't want Uncle Jack to go to sleep.

What a sport his uncle was. He began singing, and Paul joined him, both of them singing at the tops of their voices. It echoed round the cave and somehow did cheer them up.

Chapter Nine

The men on the coastguard watch had been surprised at the suddenness and severity of the storm. They looked through their telescopes and could see very few ships around Portland Bill, but when Uncle Jack sent up the flare, they had spotted the distress signal at once. They could just make out the position of the *Lady Lucy*, so they immediately alerted the Weymouth lifeboat station. The lifeboat was launched within minutes, but so fierce was the storm that it was hard for the crew to navigate the seas and reach the area as quickly as they would have liked. When they reached the boat, it was half sunk. One of the crew went aboard but reported that he could not find any people. As the skipper looked through his binoculars, he spotted Paul at the mouth of the cave, waving his sweater. It was amazing that he saw him, for the waves were so high, but the flash of red against the dark rocks and raging seas made all the difference.

The lifeboat crew steered as near as they were able and then launched their dinghy, which was powerful and fast. It reached the cave very quickly, much to the joy of the two shipwrecked fishermen. The lifeboat men praised Paul for the way he had looked after his uncle. They helped them put on their life jackets, urging them to get into the dinghy. However, Paul said he must put the blanket and tarpaulin back. He told the member of the crew who was helping him, about the case he had found at the very back of the cave.

"Don't worry about covering it again. As soon as this storm is over we will send out the marine police to take care of it. They may be very interested; it could be modern-day smugglers."

Once Paul and his uncle were safely on board the lifeboat, they were wrapped in blankets made from tinfoil and given hot drinks. Paul asked if someone could lend him a phone to tell his dad what had happened.

"I need to talk to him, son," said the skipper. "An ambulance is waiting at the harbour to take you both to the hospital in Dorchester to check you over. Your parents can meet you there."

Still wrapped in tinfoil, Paul and Uncle Jack were transferred into the ambulance, which whizzed up the main road to Dorchester, all sirens blazing. Paul would have enjoyed the adventure had not Uncle Jack looked so blue and haggard. He prayed that his uncle would be alright.

As soon as they arrived at the hospital, Uncle was taken care of by a team of doctors and nurses. Paul's parents were waiting for him, just so relieved to see he was well.

Paul had to be checked over by the medical staff and even though he felt fine, it was decided that he should stay in the hospital overnight, just to be sure. Paul had never stayed in hospital and would much rather have gone home, but his parents agreed it was for the best. They were all worried about Great-uncle Jack because his heartbeat had become irregular. He was also admitted to a ward. Once he was settled, Paul's parents were allowed to take Paul to visit him.

"Sorry, lad," he said sadly. "I never meant the day to end like this! Maybe 'tis the end of me fishing as well. I guess the *Lady Lucy* is now on bottom of the sea! At least them lobster pots release the creatures if they aren't collected in time, so they'll not die. What a way to end."

"It wasn't your fault, Uncle Jack. Even the lifeboat men said that nobody could predict that storm coming up so quickly and being so fierce. Anyway, we had a great adventure, didn't we?" said Paul.

His old uncle grinned at him. "We really did, didn't we? Anyway, you know how to bait them pots and lay 'em out. I can still teach thee to row on the Fleet sometime. Guess we have to thank them lifeboat men. We could've been ages in that cave, undiscovered. They kep' saying how well you done, laddie, keeping me moving and waving yer jumper. You're a hero, too."

"Time to get you into bed, Paul. You've had a long, tiring, exciting day. But all's well that ends well," said his mum. They kissed Uncle Jack and promised to see him the next day when they came to collect Paul. Meanwhile, Paul's father was going to drive over to Portland and lock up

Uncle's house. He promised to make everything 'shipshape' for his uncle.

Paul slept so well that night. When he woke up the next morning, he was starving. The nurses were amazed at all the toast he devoured. They were used to sick children, not a very healthy twelve-year-old. The storm had died out through the night, and the next day was bright and sunny. His mum had left clean clothes for him, so he was up and dressed and talking to the other patients when the marine police officer arrived. He wanted to talk to Paul about the cave and hear exactly what he had seen there. Paul told him, including the fact that his uncle's rowing dinghy was left in the mouth of the cave and also that he had not replaced the blanket or the tarpaulin.

"I'll go out there at once," he told Paul. "As soon as the story of your rescue gets into the news, the person to whom the case belongs may try to make sure it was not touched. I shall be very interested in what is inside the case. We have suspected for some time that smugglers may have been at work around Portland. There are several caves under the cliffs which are not seen by people, as no one is able to walk along that stretch of shore. They can only be reached by small boats that have to make their way through very narrow, rocky stretches of water. It's a good job your old uncle is such a skilled fisherman too, or you may not have made it!"

56

"I know," answered Paul. "He's amazing. He thinks this will be the end of his fishing career, though. He is very old, but none of us know quite how old he is. He never tells us."

Just before Paul's parents arrived to take him home, the skipper of the lifeboat also came to visit Paul and Uncle Jack to see how they were doing. He was pleased to see Paul so well and again praised him for his common sense. "It certainly helped to save your uncle's life," he said.

"Uncle saved mine by rowing us to the cave," Paul answered, "so we are quits, but both of us owe our lives to you and your crew. Thank you so much. Maybe when I am grown up I can join the lifeboat crew."

"That's good thinking," the skipper answered. "We certainly always need brave young men to join us."

Uncle Jack was sitting up in bed and looking his usual self again. He'd already had enough of hospital and wanted to go home. Paul's parents managed to persuade him to come back with them to the farm for at least a couple of days once the doctor would allow him to leave. His face brightened at that and also at the sight of his own clothes which Paul's dad had brought from the cottage. Paul told him about the visit from the marine policeman and also that the rowing boat would be rescued, even though the *Lady Lucy* had sunk.

When Paul arrived home, he found that Tim and Tess had gone to Live Wires. Paul was sorry to have missed it as he wanted to tell the leader how he had prayed in the storm and God had answered. Anyway, his mum sat with him in the kitchen, and he told her all about the whole adventure, including his prayer.

"It was strange because here we had some heavy rain, but no real storm. Then, as it got late we were surprised not to have heard from you. I was getting tea for everyone, and I felt a huge urge to go and pray for you. I felt something had gone wrong. Not long after I had prayed, the lifeboat skipper called and told us you had both been rescued and that we were to meet the ambulance at Dorchester Hospital. What a wonderful answer to both of our prayers. Your dad and I thanked God so much last night when we came home and knew you both were safe," said Paul's mum, wiping a tear from her eye. She hugged her son. "I don't know what I would have done if you had not been rescued."

Later that day, Uncle Jack was allowed to leave the hospital and stay at the farm. He was almost his usual self, but he did allow Mrs Jenkins to make a fuss of him as she brought him cups of tea and let him sit by the fire with his feet up. She understood that it had all been a huge shock, and he would need time to get over it. Paul, Tim and Tess were sent out for a bike ride. Tess had had a new bike for her birthday a few weeks before, and she loved to be able to cycle round the country lanes with her brothers. They all had their nature diaries with them, and Tess had her crayons because she found it much easier to draw what she saw than to spell it.

Their mum had made them a few sandwiches for a 'mini' picnic, so they decided to go to a village a few miles east of the Sydings, where there was a village duck pond. It was a nice place to sit and eat, and also there was a cycle track part of the way. As soon as they arrived, they decided they were starving and so ate their sandwiches. Next they explored the pond. Although it was only March, they were delighted to find loads of frogspawn and even some tadpoles swimming in the pond. The boys had a net and went looking for newts while Tess drew her picture. Tim found a couple of newts hiding in the mud at the bottom of the pond, so he duly noted this in his diary.

They also saw mallard and tufted ducks, moorhens and coots. The children wished they had saved the crusts from their sandwiches to feed them. Thinking of sandwiches made them realise they were hungry again, so they cycled home, knowing their mum would have made a wonderful tea.

Chapter Ten

Gran, Tyler's mum Betty and Sunshine were having a wonderful time travelling along the country lanes in Somerset. It had taken them a whole week to travel just sixty miles, but that was how they liked it. Sparks was now an old pony, and he also appreciated not going too far or too fast. Sometimes, Sunshine sat on his back as he pulled the vardo along. Gran usually had a ride, but Betty walked alongside.

Many of the farms which they passed were places which Gran had known all her life. The older farmers recognised her and welcomed her onto their land to camp for the night. They offered clean water and even the use of toilets, because they knew she could be trusted. They chatted about the old days when she used to pick heather to make into bunches and sell or made clothes pegs and sold them from door to door. Sometimes Gran had worked in their fields, picking peas when they were in season or flowers to go to the markets in London. Everything had changed over the past twenty years or so, not only for the gypsies but also for the farmers.

One of the biggest problems for the farmers were badgers who were thought to be infected with T.B. (tuberculosis). They then infected the cows, and the milk could carry the disease to humans. The cows were tested regularly, and if it was proved that they also had T.B., then they had to be killed. It was a huge loss for the farmers. Many of them wanted to kill the badgers who had setts on their land, but that wasn't allowed either. Of course, the badgers were beautiful creatures too and protected by law. One day, Gran and her family were travelling a little way inland from the coast, and they came across a sanctuary for injured badgers. Betty decided it would be a nice outing for Sunshine, so they stopped and visited. There were badgers, both big and small, in special cages so that visitors could see them even in the daytime. Badgers normally sleep through the day and come out at night to look for their food. Sunshine was thrilled to see them. Indeed, they are such beautiful creatures.

Also, there were other animals in the sanctuary including hedgehogs that had been rescued. Sunshine was able to sit with a hedgehog on her lap and feed it milk from a very tiny bottle. Gran laughed. She remembered the time when the Romany people hunted hedgehogs for food. They were wrapped in mud and baked in the embers of the fire. All the spines stuck in the mud, and so when the mud shell was opened, the meat was ready to eat and had no spines on it. Even Gran was glad that hedgehogs were no longer eaten. They were so cute, and she was glad that people were now protecting and helping them.

Sunshine so loved her visit that they spent hours at the sanctuary. Sparks had been 'parked' with the vardo in the car park, much to the amusement of other visitors. In fact, they were an attraction in themselves, and even the staff came out to see Sparks and brought him sugar lumps and apples! When they found out that the three 'girls' needed a pitch for the night, they said they were welcome to stay in the car park for several days if they liked. Sunshine certainly 'liked'. She begged Gran to stay so that she could see more of the animals in the sanctuary; in fact, she was allowed to help shut them all in for the night. Betty helped milk the goats, something she had not done for years. They were given some goats' milk, which was a real treat for them all. Most of the staff had gone home, but the owners of the sanctuary lived in a house on the site. Gran invited them to come and join them around the campfire after supper, and they were pleased to do this. Betty got out her guitar and sang some folk songs and then the special song which God had given her and her husband one night. It had been that song which had led to them becoming Christians and changing their way of living.

After she had finished singing, Gran began to tell them the story of her life as a Romany gypsy, then how everything had changed when she asked Jesus into her life to be her Saviour. When she had finished talking, her face was glowing, and it wasn't just from the warmth of the fire! Her face had lit up with happiness. She told her new friends how much she wished she had heard about Jesus and learned to love him when she was young, because her life was now so wonderful, and she explained that this trip was to visit some of her Romany relatives and tell them her story. "And it all started with the song Betty sang to you!" she said.

"Would you mind singing it again?" the owners of the sanctuary asked Betty.

"Gladly," she answered and sang it again, her sweet voice filling the evening air with music. When she finished, everyone was quiet, taking in the beautiful words.

The next day, Gran thanked their hosts very much, and they continued on their journey towards a town called Burnham-on-Sea. Gran had heard that two of her sons and their families were camping on the sand dunes. She was so excited because she would see her sons and their families, and Betty would see her brothers. It took most of the morning to reach them, but when they did, they were received with a happy, noisy reception! Betty's brothers and their families lived in caravans, but as soon as the vardo appeared, all the grandchildren rushed around to look at it and admire it! Gran was the centre of attention and was given all the respect which older people in the Romany clan should have. Sunshine was delighted to have lots of cousins with whom she could play. In the afternoon, they all went to the beach to build the biggest sandcastle she had ever seen. How she wished she could show it to Tyler and her dad.

Later on in the evening when they chatted on the phone she told them all about it.

The families had an outdoor feast together. The grown-ups helped prepare the food, and the children scoured the beach for driftwood to burn. After they had all eaten, the violins and guitars came out, and there was dancing and singing. Even passers-by stopped to watch the dancing and listen to the haunting melodies of the songs. Most of them were in the Romany language, but they were so beautiful.

Eventually, everyone sat around the embers of the fire, and many of the small children fell asleep, including Sunshine. Then the grown-ups all looked at Gran, wanting her to tell a story. Once again, she told them not only stories of her life as a traveller but also how her life had changed since she became a Christian. They all loved and respected Gran, so they knew what she was saying was true. Once again, the happiness shone out of her face! They could see too that their sister Betty had changed as well. She explained why she had given up telling fortunes, but they didn't really understand. Later, when the men had gone off drinking, she told her sisters-in-law that Bill no longer got drunk or beat her. They were very impressed at that and wanted to ask her more about her faith. They talked late into the night. In some ways they were badly treated as gypsies, chased from one site to another. They were also often hit by their husbands after they had been out drinking. They wished for better lives and wanted to know more about Jesus. Gran and Betty tried to answer all their questions. They decided to stay with them for a few days to explain more.

This was exactly what Gran had prayed for; she wanted to share with all her relatives about Jesus.

Before they left Somerset, they all went to a fair which was being held on a village common. It was an opportunity for Gran to meet up with many of her old friends. Sunshine had a great time playing on the roundabouts and rides with her cousins. One of them won a big teddy bear for her on the coconut shy. She was so pleased with it. She was missing her little kitten, so she was glad to have something new to cuddle.

Chapter Eleven

The week after his mum and gran had gone travelling, Tyler and his dad began to build the log cabin. His dad had bought the timbers needed, and since he was very used to working with wood and also a good craftsman, things began to take shape surprisingly quickly. When the next Saturday arrived, Tyler asked Theo if he would like to come and help. Theo was thrilled. Once he had looked after his chickens and ducks and also had some swimming practice, he cycled over to Honeysuckle Cottage. His mum had given him a steak and kidney pie for Tyler and his dad. She was sure they must be missing Betty's home cooking.

In fact, it wasn't just the cooking Tyler was missing. He was really missing his mum, gran and little sister. The cottage seemed so quiet without them and the yard so empty without the vardo. He missed the smell of wood smoke from Gran's fire and the smell of home-baked bread from his mum's kitchen. He missed the silly chatter of Sunshine and his helping her play games. Of course, it was really great to do 'man' things with his dad, and Tyler was very excited about the cabin, which was to be a big surprise for 'the girls' when they came home. His mum phoned every night, and when she asked what he had been doing, Tyler had to be

careful not to let the 'cat out of the bag', in other words, not
to tell them their secret.

When Theo arrived with the pie, Tyler and his dad were
delighted. They had eaten a lot of pizza and ready-made
meals and were glad of a change. They decided to keep it
for a Sunday treat.

When Theo saw the cabin, he was amazed. It was much
bigger than a 'Wendy house' and would make a fantastic club
room for their Wildlife Society. Tyler's dad, Bill, showed him
how to hold the logs in place while he nailed them together,
and with the three of them working, they made good progress.
It was hard work but huge fun to see the building grow. Theo
had never done anything like it before. If Tyler was missing
his mum, then Theo was missing having a dad living at home.
It would be so great to have a dad around to teach him how to
do 'man' things. He thought of his dad living in Australia with
his new wife and little girl. He wondered what his half-sister
was like. Was Lucy Jane as much fun as Sunshine?

His dad did ring very occasionally and sometimes sent his
mum money to help out, but he had only seen him once
since he left home. Since then, Theo had begun to email
every week but didn't always get answers, yet was thrilled to
bits when he did, but it wasn't the same as having Dad living
at home.

It was hard for his mum too, though she never complained.
Theo hoped she would get some replies for her advert for

a helper when it was given out the next day at church. He hated to see his mum so tired all the time. As he held the log in place and thought about his mum, Theo whispered a little prayer:

"Please, Father God, let someone nice want to help my mum!"

Soon it was lunch time, and Bill told the boys they all needed a break. In the kitchen he found a large loaf of bread and some cheese, and they made very man-sized sandwiches. Washed down with hot chocolate, they were very good. Tyler had promised to look after Kitty, Sunshine's little kitten, so he found her bowl and opened some cat food for her. Usually she was waiting for her meal and brushing around his legs, but today there was no sign of her. He went outside and called her name, but no Kitty arrived. Puzzled, Tyler told his dad, and together the three of them searched the cottage in case she had got herself shut into a room or cupboard. She was a very playful kitten and always getting into scrapes. There was just no sign of her, and they began to get worried.

"Dad, I think we should go out and hunt for her in the woods," said Tyler. His dad agreed. "Kitty has been missing Sunshine; maybe she has gone looking for her," he said.

Honeysuckle Cottage was situated on the edge of the woods of which Bill was the manager, so he knew every inch of them. The 'Two T's' and Bill started to hunt through the extensive woods, calling for the kitten as they went. They met a couple who were out walking with their dog and asked them if they had seen a kitten. Unfortunately, they hadn't and said their dog would certainly let them know if there was a cat anywhere near as he always chased them.

Bill glanced up at the sky. "It looks like a storm is brewing. I don't like the look of that sky," he said.

Tyler was looking very miserable.

"I promised Sunshine I would take care of Kitty. She loves her so much. What will I say if we can't find her?" he said, looking at his dad.

"We've forgotten something," said Theo. "We haven't asked God to help us find her."

"You're right," answered Bill. "That's the first thing we should have thought of."

The three of them stopped, and Bill simply asked God to take care of Kitty, wherever she was, and also to lead them to her.

For about an hour, they searched in the woods without any success. Tyler was beginning to despair again. They sat down on a fallen tree trunk for a rest, and Theo noticed a little clump of fur nearby.

"Isn't that like Kitty's fur?" he asked. Theo also had a kitten who was the brother of Kitty, so he recognised the colouring.

"I think it is," said Bill. "That means she has come this way. She may have got caught in the brambles or fallen into a hole. Come on, let's look around."

They started searching again, and then Tyler thought
he heard a mewing. They all stopped and listened. Yes, it
definitely was a cat. It was hard to hear where the mewing
was coming from, but Theo was sure it was from above
them. They called out "Kitty, Kitty" and waited for her
reply. As they listened, they could hear a mewing which was
coming from the trees. Then Tyler saw her, way out on one
of the top branches. She had gone so far she wasn't able to
jump down and looked very small and frightened.

"Dad, may I climb up and get her?" asked Tyler. He felt
very responsible for the kitten.

"Definitely not!" replied his father. "Even I cannot climb
that tree without proper equipment. This is a job for the Fire
Brigade!"

Bill pulled his mobile from his pocket and dialled 999.
Soon he was talking to the fireman and explaining the
situation.

"No problem," was the answer, "but it may take us about
twenty minutes to reach you. It's not easy through the
country lanes, let alone Syding Woods!"

It was almost exactly twenty minutes later when the fire
brigade arrived. The engine just about made it down the
track through the woods. They ran their very long ladders
into the tree, and an officer climbed up, wearing ropes to
keep him safe. Finally, he reached the poor terrified kitten
and brought her safely down to the boys.

When Tyler took her, he saw she had been chased by an animal and that lumps of her fur were missing. His dad thought maybe a big dog had chased her. Her skin was not broken as far as he could see, so he decided she didn't need to go to the vet.

They thanked the fire crew for all their help. They laughed and said that rescuing kittens was all part of their day's work.

The 'Two T's' and Bill took the kitten back to the cottage, and once she was inside and saw her plate of food, she began to eat as if she hadn't eaten for weeks.

"She'll be alright now," remarked Bill. "Her adventure hasn't put her off her food!"

It was too late to start working on the log cabin again, so the boys played a computer game for a while before it was time to go home. The storm had now broken, and it was pouring with rain and blowing a gale, so Bill put Theo's bike in his car and drove him home. It gave him and Tyler a chance to say thank you for the wonderful pie Theo's mum had sent them. Thinking of that reminded Bill that they should say thank you to God for keeping Kitty safe and helping them to find her, so when he arrived at the castle and stopped the engine, they did just that. They were all so grateful for the return of the kitten both safe and sound.

Chapter Twelve

The Live Wires meeting at church the next day was quite exciting. First of all, Tim and Tessa wanted to tell everyone about Paul's rescue from the fishing boat. It made the rescue of Kitty seem quite tame in comparison! Theo and the twins wanted to talk about the young couple who had stayed with them the previous weekend and who were working in Burundi.

"It is the poorest country in the whole world!" Seb told them. "That is worked out by how much money there is for each person or something like that. Anyway, after a thirteen-year civil war, many refugees are returning and own nothing and have nowhere to go."

"There are even mothers and children who try to make a shelter on the streets," added Flick. "The whole country is in a state of poverty."

"We thought it would be a good idea, if you agree," said Theo, looking at the leader and co-leaders of the group, "if we did some fundraising in the Easter holidays to help these people. Do you think we could?"

The young people in the group looked really interested and excited, and the leader said he thought it would be a fantastic idea. He reminded them that again and again in the Bible, God's people are told to care for the widows and orphans and the poor, because God cares about their situation.

They began to think of ideas, and their leader wrote them up on a whiteboard.

"Mum says we can use the swimming pool for a 'swimathon'," Theo said, "but she can't be responsible. Anyone coming needs a parent with them, and we really should have a trained lifeguard."

"It's a wonderful idea," said the leader as he wrote it on the board. "I have a friend who has a lifesaving certificate. I'll talk to him and see if he would help us. We would need to work out the fine details of sponsoring when I get his reply."

"I can't swim," complained one lad, and a couple of others said the same.

"I thought of that," said Seb. "We could have a 'round the table' table tennis marathon for those who don't want to swim. We can hold both events at the same time."

"Another great idea," the leader said, and wrote that one down too.

Tess was always a bit shy as she was the youngest in the group. However, she had been thinking and knew her mum would help.

"I think we should have a cake stall. We could all make some cakes and cookies or even sweets and sell them on the village green on a Saturday morning. I know Mum will help."

That was written up. Soon the ideas came fast and furious. Some wanted a sponsored bike ride, others thought they could have a toys and games sale of things they no longer used but were in a good condition.

One of the junior leaders thought a 'snowball' would be fun.

"What do you mean, 'a snowball'?" asked Mia, Tess's friend.

"Well," explained the leader, "I would give each of you a set amount of money, possibly three pounds. With this money you buy materials and then make something which you can sell for a profit. With the profit you then buy more materials and so you continue to make your money grow like a snowball. I could give the money to you at the start of the holidays, and we could collect in all the profits at the beginning of the summer term. What do you think?"

"It sounds like the story in the Bible of the talents!" Tyler remarked.

"What's that story?" asked Flick. The leader told them all to turn in their Bibles to St Matthew, chapter 25 and verses 14 to 29. They talked a lot about what Jesus meant when he told the story and also about the different gifts which they all had and how they could use them for God.

"I see!" said Tim. "It's like Tess being able to draw and paint. She can use her money to buy paper and maybe a frame for a picture and then sell it so next time she makes two!"

"Exactly," said the leader. "That's a good example, Tim. Tess has a gift for drawing, and I know I would like to buy one of her pictures!" Tess beamed at that.

They all began to think of things which they could make and sell. Some who couldn't think of anything were given ideas by others in the group, and one or two decided to have joint projects. It looked as if they would all have very busy Easter holidays! The final good idea came from Flick.

"It's hard selling things one by one. Once we have grown our money a bit, why don't we have a big 'splash' and have a Village Live Wires Market on May Bank Holiday? We could advertise it and have stalls for some of the other things we suggested like a toy stall and a cake stall. I'm sure Theo's hens will be pleased to lay some eggs, and we should have something growing in our veggie patch, even if it's only rhubarb!"

By the time the grown-ups had come out of church, everyone was bubbling with ideas and running to tell their parents about the 'market' they planned to hold as well as the other events!

Theo's mum was also beaming and wanting to share some good news. Two people had come and told her that they would love to help her at the castle with the bed and breakfast guests. One was a girl called Jenny who was in her last year at college and really wanted a holiday job. Helping at the castle would be ideal because she would still have time to study. Sally knew her a little and thought she would be good company for Penny, even though she was a bit older. It was quite hard for Penny in the school holidays as being at a boarding school meant she had fewer friends in the village.

The other lady who asked to be considered was called Annie. She was a trained secretary whose job had just finished. She would be very glad of work while she looked for another job. Sally didn't really know Annie because she had been working in Bristol but now had come back to her parents' home until she got another job. Both Jenny and Annie were coming to see her in the morning to talk about the job. That gave Sally the rest of the day to think and pray about who should help her.

On the way home, she told her children that they could all go to the Live Wires weekend, and they whooped in delight! They had not had any holiday since their father left them. Before that they had gone to many exciting places around the world, but these holidays were just distant memories.

As soon as they arrived home, they rang the leader and asked him to put their names on the list!

Chapter Thirteen

On the morning bus to school, the 'Two T's' and the twins were eager to hear Paul tell them all about his adventure on Saturday. The school bus always arrived in good time, and this allowed Paul to make his way to the prayer space which the school had made available for any pupil or member of staff who wished to use it. He quietly thanked God for his rescue and also that his Great-uncle Jack seemed his old self again. Then he renewed his commitment to the Lord Jesus, asking him to be in complete control of his life. It seemed to him that his life must have been saved for a reason, and he asked Jesus to help him to know what he should do when he was grown up, if he wasn't to be a farmer.

The morning lessons were uneventful, and in the lunch break the 'Faith is Fun' (FIF) group met. The 'Two T's' and Paul went whenever they could, but Seb and Flick went only occasionally. Today, however, they were all there. When they were chatting together with some of the other members, Seb began to tell them about the ideas they had come up with for fundraising for refugees in Burundi. The other FIF's members seemed not only interested but they also wanted to join in and help. They even had some ideas of their own.

Seb was thrilled. With the extra help, they should be able to raise a lot of money.

Towards the end of the afternoon, the head of year seven came to find Paul and asked him to go with him to the headmaster's office. Paul was scared. He wondered if there had been a complaint about his language on the bus or something like that. He prayed silently for courage to be brave and truthful.

When he reached the headmaster's office, he was greeted by the head. "Don't look so scared, Paul. We just want to share some good news with you before the whole school hears it!"

Inside the office was the marine policeman whom he had seen in the hospital.

"Hello, Paul," he said, "I wanted you to be the first to hear the good news! As soon as I left you on Sunday morning, as I promised, I went to the cave. I found it easily because of your uncle's dinghy being there. It is safe and sound, by the way. I towed it back to Chiswell and secured it at his mooring. Anyway, I explored the cave, finding the rug and tarpaulin and there, as you described it, was the case. I had tools with me and opened it. It was as I had suspected: a modern-day smuggler's haul. It was full of plastic bags of heroin. They have been tested this morning in the police lab, and it is very high grade stuff, worth thousands of pounds on the open market. For sometime we have been aware that drug smuggling has been happening in the area, but this haul is just amazing!

"In case you are wondering what happens next, I locked the case, which now contains bags of flour, covered it with the tarpaulin, and my undercover men are on a twenty-four-hour watch of the cave. We hope we will soon have the smuggler where he should be, under lock and key!"

"Wow! That's amazing," said Paul, "and thank you for telling me and for taking care of Uncle's rowing boat. I guess he's lost his fishing boat, hasn't he?"

"Yes, I'm afraid so, son," the policeman told him. "We have sent someone out to pick up the lobster pots and buoys, though. If there are lobsters, shall I get them sold at the fish market? That would seem the most sensible thing to do."

"Thank you, sir," replied Paul. "Since it is the last catch of the season, maybe it will be some money for Uncle Jack. He was thinking he ought to give it all up. He is very old, but none of us quite know just how old!"

"Now, Paul," continued the policeman, "we will allow the news to be released about the lifeboat rescue in the storm, but say nothing about the drugs haul until we catch the criminal, so please still keep it quiet. When the whole thing is wrapped up, then the headmaster has invited me to come and talk to everyone at assembly about the dangers of drug abuse. Would you be willing to tell your side of the story when that happens?"

"Yes, of course, if you think it will help," answered Paul. "Anyway, I would like to tell everyone how wonderful the lifeboat crew were. Without them, we might not have been rescued for a long time, and I don't think Uncle Jack would have survived!"

Paul was so glad to be able to tell Great-uncle Jack the news about his rowing boat and the lobster pots when he arrived home from school.

"I've decided," Uncle Jack said, "that I shall never fish again. *Lady Lucy* were well insured, and I shall put in a claim. The pots can be sold. They cost about £60.00 each. 'Tis kind of the police to sell them lobsters for us. They'll probably make a few bob. 'Tis hard gettin' old, but 'tis a good life I've had. No, I can't complain. Did I ever tell thee 'bout the time when I were young, fishing on the Fleet?"

Paul smiled encouragingly. Yes, Uncle Jack had told him many times before, but he loved to hear the stories over and over.

"I was 'bout ten year old," Uncle Jack began, "and at weekend I'd be sent out to Chickerell, to me old gran. Me cousin Alfie twoud be there, and he and I were same age and good friends. His dad, me Uncle Tom, twoud be out with his mates in the lerret—that be a flat-bottomed boat used on the Fleet for fishin'. Alfie and I had to row out to them in a little boat called a trow, taking their canteen of cold tea which Gran had made 'em. Then, we had to row back the catch of mackerel what they'd caught. All the fish were in the bottom of the trow, 'round our feet. I tell thee, lad, twere right smelly! When we got on shore at Chickerell, t'other uncle, Uncle Sam, were waiting, and he'd pack 'em into boxes. Thirty-six fish to a box, in crushed ice.

"I remember one time there were over four thousand fish! Alfie and I had to go runnin' to Weymouth to get more ice. T'were in huge blocks and were put in to sacks, so then we 'ad to go to a place in the old High Street West where they 'ad a crushing machine and then take it all way back up to Chickerell. We weren't runnin' then! I tell thee, 'twere a heavy load and cold for a ten year old!"

"What happened to all that fish?" Paul asked his uncle.

"Oh, laddie, it 'ad to be loaded onto cart and taken to station. We 'ad to get it there in time for early trains to Bristol and London! By time it 'twere gone, we'd tired ourselves right out! We were used to gettin' up early, but them Saturdays we were up before dawn! 'Twere great fun, though, and Alfie and me enjoyed it all. We even earned a penny or two sometimes for our labours. At Christmas, t'uncles would give us both a treat. I once had an orange!"

It always amazed Paul when he heard this story to realise what a luxury an orange was. Now his mum had oranges in the fruit bowl all the time.

After a few days staying and being spoilt at Castle View Farm, Great-uncle Jack wanted to go back to his cottage.

"There be no place like your own 'ome," he told them all. "Me own old armchair, 'tis fair worn out, but so comfy! Not that I'm not real grateful to thee all, and I'll come soon and see thee, but I want to be back in me own 'ome."

So Mr Jenkins drove him home one day after he had finished the milking. Mrs Jenkins had baked all sorts of nice things to fill his fridge and larder, and they promised to visit very soon.

By the end of the week after the rescue, Paul was asked once again to go to the head's office. This time he wasn't scared; he just hoped the police had caught the smuggler. It was indeed good news! Two men had been caught red-handed as they tried to retrieve the case. They had no idea it was filled with flour! When they saw their game was up, they gave in without any great struggle and were now safely locked up waiting for a court appearance. Not only was the marine policeman there but also the skipper of the lifeboat. They asked Paul if he was up to talking in assembly not just about finding the case but also about keeping his uncle warm and moving in the cave. He felt a bit uncomfortable about that, for he was no great hero, but when the skipper said it might make more young people aware of how easily old folk can get cold, he agreed.

The assembly was at the end of Friday afternoon. Paul found it all a bit nerve-racking and didn't want to be made out as a hero. He loved his great uncle and just wanted him to be alright, so he tried to explain this.

However, the skipper did praise him for his common sense and especially for not just taking care of his uncle but also for waving his red sweater, which made it easier for the lifeboat crew to see him.

It was not so bad telling the story of how he had walked around the cave and found the case. Anyone in that situation would have wanted to explore!

The policeman talked about the temptations and dangers of using drugs and even why some people ended up as drug pushers because of the huge amount of money to be made that way. Although they had all heard the messages about drugs before, somehow this time, because of the local adventure, it made a great impact on the young people.

After assembly was finished, the head stopped and told Paul that he was very proud of him and that he had spoken up really well. Even the people at the back of the hall had heard.

"Maybe you'll end up being a teacher like me!" he joked.

"I wonder," replied Paul thoughtfully.

Chapter Fourteen

*I*t had been a good week at the castle too. On Monday, the two ladies who wanted to work there came to see Theo's mum, Sally. She liked them both very much and thought both would be really good workers. She didn't know who to choose! She told them she would phone the next day, and once they had gone, she talked to God about the problem.

"Both these women need work, dear Lord. Who should I ask to help?" she prayed.

In her mind the words "Employ both of them, you will be busy!" kept going round and round. She decided it must be God speaking to her, and although it didn't make financial sense, Sally decided to do just that. She phoned both ladies and offered them work, also asking Annie if she would help with some of the office work as Jenny would be there to help with the guests. It was almost the Easter holidays, so both ladies agreed to start work the following Monday. This would help them to get to know their way around, ready for the busy time at Easter. The bedrooms were all booked already, some guests being the archaeological team from Oxford who were booked to continue their work excavating the Roman site in the grounds.

Seb had a wonderful week organizing all the fundraising events. His mum laughed when she thought about it! He was so like his father, who was a very successful businessman and always very good at organizing things! She was sure that one day he would end up in business and be very good at making money too. She hoped he would continue to do it to help other people who were worse off than himself.

For Flick, things were not so good. Sally sighed when she thought about her younger daughter. Now that Sparks, the pony, was pulling the vardo all over the country, Flick was a bit lost. She adored horses and spent time every day riding and grooming Sparks. Of course, Flick knew that he belonged to Tyler's gran and that maybe she would go travelling again, but she had secretly hoped it wouldn't happen. Flick always seemed to live in the shadow of Seb, happy to be organised by him and do whatever he wanted her to do. Her mum knew that one day Seb would make his own way in the world, and she wanted Flick to be confident to do the same. At school she was neither very good nor very bad at anything, just average. There was nothing wrong with that, of course, but Sally wished there was something special that she could encourage her daughter to do. Penny, her oldest daughter, was so different, being really gifted in music and now at a music academy boarding school in Manchester. Penny had been sure of what she wanted to be from a very early age and was always focused and working to achieve her dream.

Then there was Theo. His mum had no real worries about her youngest son. He was only eleven but was good at sport, loved the natural world and seemed to be getting an interest in farming. He certainly took the care of his chickens very seriously and consulted Mr Jenkins about them. Theo, too, was very focused. Since Amy and Dan had stayed with them, he had practiced his butterfly stroke over and over, perfecting the tips which Amy had given him. The inter-schools' swimming gala was only a week away, and he was determined to do his very best! Two of the schools in the district were specialist sports schools, and so the Dorchester High School found it hard to do well. The football season was drawing to an end, but their team had been knocked out of the championship long ago. The hockey team had done little better, and the netball team were knocked out in the quarter finals. Somehow, it was discouraging for all the sports teams, including the swimming squad. Yet Theo had great determination and loved the Bible story about David defeating the mighty Goliath. He prayed that God would help him to do really well, beating his own personal best!

As well as swimming, Theo had another hobby. He loved going out with his metal detector. Usually he only found buried rubbish rather than treasure, but it was such fun. Through the winter he had not done much, partly because the days were short, but also because the ground was so hard. Since the archaeological team had gone back to Oxford, he'd had several finds of Roman coins up near the site where the team were excavating. He kept them to show the professor when he returned. He had also found a couple of metal buttons which looked as if they might have belonged on a military uniform, and these were put away too. He wanted to take them into Dorchester and ask the curator of the museum if he had any ideas. He had always been so helpful in the past, especially when he and Tyler had discovered the pirate's pistol in the autumn. The wreck where they found it was due to be explored in the Easter holidays, and he was looking forward to that. Theo just hoped it wouldn't clash with the time when the Live Wires were away.

On Saturday that week, the Wildlife Society met at Honeysuckle Cottage. This meant they could all see the progress on the log cabin. It would make a fantastic meeting place for them all! It was really going up very quickly because now that the evenings were a bit lighter, Tyler and his dad could work for an hour or so. The walls were all in place, and so were the beams necessary for taking the roofing timbers. Somehow just being inside was wonderful with the smell of new wood! They knew they would share it with Sunshine, too. She would use it as a playhouse, but Tyler's dad had promised to make a cupboard with a padlock, just for their use, so that Sunshine wouldn't use it on club days. They all promised to come back and help in the afternoon because Paul had a project for them that morning. He had jam jars and fishing nets and wanted them to go to the next village pond and collect some frog and toad spawn for the new lake at the castle. He explained to them all that frogs and toads always go back to the place where they were spawned to lay their eggs. So, in order to populate the new lake with frogs and toads, they needed to 'import' some spawn. Everyone agreed it would be great fun. They all had bikes, so it didn't take long to get there.

It took longer to get the spawn, though! They had to be careful not to fall into the pond, especially since the spawn always seemed just out of reach. There were lots of laughs, especially when Tim slipped on the side of the pond and ended up with a very muddy backside! As well as spawn, they caught some tadpoles too. Tess wanted to take hers home to watch them grow into tiny frogs, but everyone else said they would put theirs in the pond. The cycle ride back to the castle was rather slow; nobody wanted to tip up their jam jar! Somehow they managed, and they all trooped up the castle drive, thrilled with their morning's work.

By now it was past lunchtime, but Theo, Seb and Flick's mum had made a huge pile of sandwiches. They had phoned her to say they would be late. She was always glad that they took their mobiles with them on their expeditions;

at least she usually knew where they were and what they were up to! The children ate hungrily, then plodded up the hill to the new lake and one by one emptied their jam jars into the water. Tess in the end decided not to take hers home after all and did the same.

Before they went back to help Tyler's dad, the club had an important thing to do. Kayla, Tess's best friend, wanted to join the club. Everyone had agreed, but the children had decided to make badges for themselves. Tess, being by far the best artist, had designed a badge with a little frog on it. Flick had produced a badge-making machine that she had been given years before as a birthday present but never used. They made really nice badges, and Tess took Kayla's to give to her at school on Monday. She wasn't always able to come to meetings but hoped to come in the school holidays when she had sleepovers with Tess.

The boys all went down to help Bill with the log cabin while Flick and Tess had a discussion about things they would need, like cushions and cups. It was all very exciting.

Chapter FIFteen

The day of the swimming gala was drizzly, and wet fog hung over all the villages. It was the sort of day that made you think about November, not March! Nevertheless, Theo woke so excited about the gala that nothing was going to dampen his spirits! His gear was already packed, including the new shorts his mum had bought. She had made arrangements for her new employee, Annie, to meet the couple who were coming to stay the night and settle them in, so that she could watch her son swim.

The school day seemed to drag for Theo. His mind was definitely on other things! At lunch time it was the FIF's meeting, and he went along as usual. He asked the group to pray for him that he would not get an attack of nerves but would do the very best he could. He would have liked his mates to pray that he would win, but he wasn't sure that was a very fair thing to do. He was pleased though, because most of his friends were able to come and cheer for him and the squad.

When the afternoon lessons had finished, the swimming squad met in the school sports' centre and were given a high energy snack and drink. The head of department for sports talked to them all, encouraging them to do their best and thanking them for all the hard work they had done to prepare for the gala. He ran through a few things, reminding them all of the order of the races and who was in the relay teams and which leg followed which. He was aware that with all the stress and excitement of the event, such things were easily forgotten.

The boys and girls were taken by coach to the town leisure centre where the gala was to take place. Most of them were familiar with it as they had been there to practice and train as a team. Soon they were changed and waiting for their races. There were many children around from different schools, all excited and shivering a bit in anticipation.

When they went to the poolside, they were given front seats to sit in while they waited for their own race.

Theo saw that all the stands were full with spectators. He looked round to see if he could see his mum, the twins and Tyler. It took ages to find them, but when they saw him they all waved madly. He saw that Paul, Tim and Tess were watching, too. He wished that Penny could have been there, but she hadn't yet broken up from school. His mum had her camera phone and had promised to video his race to send to Penny, his dad and also Amy and Dan. He must do well for them! He wanted them all to feel proud of him!

The sense of excitement began to mount as the races started! All the spectators were cheering and clapping and yelling for their friends and family. Theo had to wait for quite a long time before the boys' under-thirteen butterfly race was announced. Talk about butterflies! His stomach was full of them!

He quietly prayed in his head for God to calm him, and then he entered the pool to take his marks. He was in a middle lane, which quite pleased him. The minute the starting whistle was blown, Theo remembered Amy's instructions of how important it was to make a good strong stroke to start, and he shot through the water. Unaware of the contestants around him, he swam the length, made a fantastic turn and with every ounce of power he could muster, completed the second length. He could hear 'Theo, Theo, Theo,' being chanted and a huge cheer as he touched the side. It took him a few minutes to realise that he had not only achieved a personal best, but he had also won the race by a whole stroke!

The sports teacher helped him out of the water, congratulating him on his achievement.

"To think this isn't your best stroke and you only volunteered because nobody else did! I am so very proud of you and pleased by your performance!" he said. "You are a credit to the school, and I shall have my eye on you from now on. I'll have you swimming for the county before you leave school."

Wrapped in his towel and no longer shaking with nerves, Theo looked up to the stand where his family and friends were sitting. He waved to them and they shouted back, "Well done Theo!"

However, he knew that he couldn't relax yet. There was still the medley relay to come. He was tired already and so tried to take deep breaths and focus again on the remaining task ahead. This time it wasn't too long to wait for his team's turn. The younger students went before the older ones in the relays. When it came his turn once again, he made a huge effort and pulled away quickly from his competitors. The change over was good, and the school team did very well, coming in second. Everyone was delighted! Others in the school team had also done well in their individual races, although Theo was the only winner. At the end, there was a presentation and he proudly received a gold medal for the butterfly race and a silver one for the team medley. The competitors then went to get changed and rejoin their families. As he went he whispered a big 'thank you' to God for helping him.

Theo's mum was talking to the head of sport. He was telling her that Theo was a credit to them all and because of all his hard work his stroke had improved very much.

"That's what Theo is like," his mum said proudly. "If he sets his mind to do something, he will work and work at it and really do his best. I'm very proud of him and thrilled for him!"

Theo's mum treated them all to a meal at a pizza restaurant in Dorchester before they drove home. Theo was very tired after all the effort but so elated. He was glad his mum had made a video of the race. He knew that Amy's coaching had made such a difference too, so he wanted to email and thank her. However, all that had to wait until the next day!

In fact, the excitement wasn't quite over because in the school assembly the next day all the swimming team had to go on to the platform and be congratulated and cheered for their success the previous evening. The school had not done so well in a gala for years! Theo was given special mention and awarded points for his house! The head of sport mentioned how Theo had volunteered when no one else wanted to enter the butterfly race, even though it had not been his favourite stroke.

With the swimming gala over, all Theo could think about was the end of term and the Easter holidays. He was so looking forward to seeing his big sister again but also to the Live Wires weekend away. They were going to a campsite in the New Forest.

Chapter Sixteen

On the first Friday of the Easter holidays, a very excited group of young people gathered in the Much Syding Church car park, ready for the Live Wires Adventure Weekend. There were seven boys and five girls, plus four leaders who clambered into the hired minibus, plus a huge amount of gear.

The younger Live Wires who were still at junior school looked a bit mournful as they waved off the seniors, but they were scheduled to have a week of fun at a holiday club very soon.

It had been years since Seb, Flick and Theo had been away on a holiday, and Paul and Tyler could not remember ever going away except to visit relatives very occasionally. They were determined to make the most of the next few days!

It was in fact Good Friday, and they had all been at church in the morning. This had been followed by refreshments which included hot cross buns. The vicar wanted as many of the church members as possible to be present when the young people started their journey. He gathered them all round the minibus and prayed that everyone would have a safe and happy time and also that they would all learn more about Jesus throughout the Easter weekend.

The drive to the New Forest took just over an hour. That was long enough for the excited youngsters! They couldn't wait to get out, pitch their tents on the campsite and then explore. It didn't take long to get the tents up. The site was very modern and had good toilet and cooking facilities plus a barn where meetings could be held if it was wet. They helped unload all the food and cooking gear into the kitchen and then all the games equipment into the barn. In fact, it was a lovely afternoon, not too hot and not too cold. A paper chase had been prepared, and so the youngsters and one leader set off hiking around the area 'chasing' the paper markers. It was good because they were able to get their bearings and also rid themselves of a lot of spare energy. While the paper chase was in progress, the other leaders set up a volleyball net and prepared a meal.

Tyler was completely in his element! The New Forest was one huge nature reserve, and he wanted to see everything he could. He had read that there were five species of deer in the forest: Roe, Red, Fallow, Sika and Muntjac, but the latter were rarely seen as they hide away in the denser woodland. How he would love to see one of them! They were trekking through the thicker woodland on the paper chase, but everyone was rushing around so noisily he knew that they were unlikely to see any animals and certainly not shy deer!

The game finished with everyone ending up back at the campsite, where a welcome meal was waiting for them! The

Live Wires had four tents. In one three boys and an officer were to sleep and in the other four boys with another adult. Then the other side of the campsite had two girls' tents, one for three of them and the other only two, but each had an adult as well. They found names had been fixed on each tent: Kingfisher, Nightjar, Woodlark and Firecrest. These were the names of four of the rarer species of birds found in the forest. After the meal had finished, the Nightjars were told it was their turn to wash the dishes. There was to be a competition between the four tents, and marks could be gained by doing jobs well, besides winning games, etc. No one minded helping; it was fun to do things like that at camp!

One of the girls' leaders knew a lot about the area, so in the barn she gave out some quiz sheets which the young people could fill in throughout the weekend. She told them the history of the New Forest, which wasn't really new at all. She also explained what a special place it was because it contained not only the ancient unenclosed woodlands but also valley bogs or mires as they are called, heathlands and even seashore areas. Many very unusual and rare plants grew in the habitat, including fifteen types of orchids. The Live Wires were really surprised to learn that. Some of them didn't know that any orchids grew in England; they thought they all came from exotic places overseas and were sold in garden centres and supermarkets.

When Theo heard there were more than forty types of butterflies and twenty-seven types of dragonflies, he gave a gasp of surprise. He wondered how many dragonflies might colonise the new lake in the castle grounds. He didn't know there were so many kinds.

The four tents split up to form two equal teams to play volleyball. It was a new game to most of them but huge fun. They would have gone on playing until it was dark, but the leaders had built a campfire in the centre of the site and called them all over for supper to be followed by evening prayers.

"It's like being at your house," Theo said to Tyler. "I love eating outside your gran's vardo."

"Everything tastes so much better when it is eaten outside," agreed Tyler, "but I do miss Gran and Mum and Sunshine so much. They don't seem to know when they will come home."

"I'm sure they will return home soon," Theo told his friend, hoping to cheer him up.

It was their tent's turn to clear up, so they along with Paul and another boy called James made their way over to the kitchen.

While they did the dishes, Tyler taught them a Romany song. It was a round, so once they had the tune and words in their heads they sang it as a four-part round. One of the leaders came in and was surprised at how well they were singing.

"I think you should teach this at the campfire so that we can all sing it!" he said. "But what does it mean?"

"'Mandi's the drom' means 'I am the way'."

"'Mandi's the tatchipen' means 'I am the truth'."

"'Mandi's the jivapen' means 'I am the life'."

"'Drom, tatchipen ta jivapen' means 'the way, truth and life'."

"Wow! That is cool!" the young leader exclaimed. "I am talking at prayers this evening on that very verse from John fourteen, verse six! I was going to teach a song in English which goes like this:

'I am the way, the truth and the life, that's what Jesus said,
I am the way, the truth, and the life, that's what Jesus said.
Without the way there is no going,
Without the truth there is no knowing,
Without the life there is no living,
I am the way, the truth and the life, that's what Jesus said.'

"Now we can sing in Romany and English! Where did you learn your song, Tyler?" he asked.

"My dad composed it to teach us the Bible," replied Tyler. "Mum, Dad, Gran and I sing the parts, but now Sunshine likes to join in as well. She gets very muddled, but it doesn't matter. Dad says she's praising the Lord in her own way!"

The Live Wires sat around the embers of the campfire. It was a lovely still night. They could see the stars and the moon. The young leader spoke to them all about the first Good Friday and why it was called 'good' even though Jesus was so cruelly executed. He explained so clearly that Jesus was dying instead of all the people in the world who ever had and who ever will live, that we all deserved to be on that cross as a punishment for all the wrong things we have done and will do. He told them Jesus gladly took the punishment for us so that He could be the way for us to be forgiven and go to heaven.

Everyone was quiet. It was so meaningful to hear the story sitting under the stars. Then the boys were asked to sing the Romany round. It sounded amazing in the still night air. Tyler explained what the words meant, and they all sang it, each tent taking a line. Afterwards they learned and sang the English song and then prayed to thank God for sending Jesus to be their Saviour.

It was a subdued group who went to sleep that night as they thought of the meaning of Jesus' death.

In his tent, Seb stayed awake for a long time. It was as if someone had switched on a light in his head that evening and at last he understood what Jesus had done for him. His mind kept swirling with thoughts of the wrong things he had done, maybe not in the criminal sense, but certainly he had lied and stolen, been unkind and unhelpful. It was as if Jesus was shining a torch inside his heart, the 'real Seb', showing him all of these things. It was the early hours of Saturday morning before he finally fell asleep.

Saturday was a bit of a foggy start. It took quite a bit of waking and shaking to get everyone out of their sleeping bags and up and dressed for breakfast. Once they arrived in the kitchen, the wonderful smell of bacon frying quickly revived them all! The masses of porridge, bacon and eggs and toast soon vanished, and everyone was full of energy again for the new day.

They were going on an outing in the minibus to Buckler's Hard and Lymington. A team from one of the girls' tents were helping to prepare packed lunches for them all to take with them while others were clearing up from breakfast. A tent inspection then followed. The points gained from this were not very many, but Flick's tent did the best.

Chapter Seventeen

On the way to the little hamlet of Buckler's Hard, the minibus stopped at a riding stable. This was a surprise to the Live Wires, and Flick was absolutely delighted! There were New Forest ponies and other horses to ride or just to admire and groom. Flick, Seb, Theo and Tyler were all used to riding, as were a couple of others in the group, so they were kitted out with hard hats and boots and were taken out on a pony trek, while some of the others decided to have a lesson in the management of the stables. There was no one who wasn't interested in having a ride of some sort, and in fact everyone so enjoyed themselves that it was hard to leave the stable and go back to the bus and move on to Buckler's Hard.

By the time they arrived, the sun had broken through and it was perfect for a picnic down by the river's edge. It was such a lovely little hamlet with its row of Georgian cottages that it was hard to visualise that it had been the centre of boat building for the Royal Navy in previous generations.

The boys were particularly interested in the history, as many of Lord Nelson's fleet had been built there, including the HMS Euryalus, HMS Swiftsure and Nelson's own first command and favourite ship, HMS Agamenon, all of which fought at the battle of Trafalgar in 1805.

Paul loved history; it was one of his favourite subjects at school, and he spent ages looking around the small museum. One of the Live Wires' leaders joined him.

"Did you know that this was an important place in the Second World War?" he asked Paul.

"No, I had no idea!" answered Paul. "I thought the River Beaulieu was silted up and this village was just left as a quaint reminder of the past!"

"Not at all," the leader told him. "These little shipyards were used to build motor torpedo boats. Then they were used as a base for hundreds of landing craft which were used for the Normandy invasion!"

"Wow!" exclaimed Paul. "I bet the Germans never expected them to be in such a tiny place. They bombed the big ports and shipyards, didn't they?"

"Yes, it was a very clever move. God really protected this country through the war, especially when Churchill called the nation to pray. God had mercy on us. It was only His goodness that saved us."

Then they discovered something else which Paul didn't know. They read about Sir Francis Chichester, the first person to sail around the world single-handed. After he had finished his epic journey, he returned to Buckler's Hard where he moored his boat, *Gypsy Moth IV*, and received a tremendous welcome from the villagers there.

103

The final part of the trip was to visit the small port of Lymington. The girls were pleased because there were some shops where they could browse, but the boys were more interested in the yachts in the three marinas. Some of the yachts were absolutely magnificent! They also wanted to hear about the smuggling history of the town. Sitting on the harbour wall and looking over to the Isle of Wight on that sunny afternoon, they tried to imagine the smugglers who used the tunnels running under the high street from every inn down to the quay. It reminded Tyler and Theo of the time when they had been trapped in a smugglers' tunnel in Portland. That had been a really exciting adventure!

"You know," remarked Theo, "we promised to go and visit that nice old lady who lived in Pennsylvania Castle. We've never done it. Maybe we ought to go out there this holiday." Tyler agreed it would be a good idea. There were so many interesting places to explore in Portland, another trip there would be good.

It had been a really fun day, and everyone had enjoyed themselves. They sang in the minibus as they drove back to the campsite. The favourite was Tyler's Romany round. It started Seb thinking again and feeling bad about the wrong things in his life. He knew that Jesus was speaking to him, but Seb had always loved to organise and be in control. He wasn't quite sure that he wanted to hand his life over to Jesus.

That evening the campfire prayers were shorter as everyone was so tired and they all needed to get up early the next day for an Easter sunrise service. Their tent officers promised to wake them all in good time so that they could celebrate Jesus' resurrection in this special way.

It was exciting creeping out of their sleeping bags and getting up just before dawn on Easter Sunday morning. They could imagine what the women felt when they got up early to take spices to the tomb to embalm Jesus and the excitement of seeing angels and hearing that Jesus was alive!

Well wrapped up, the young people went to a quiet part of the forest and sat on some fallen tree trunks. They had a very simple service, singing a few Easter songs and hearing the story first of the women and then the disciples going to the tomb and the wonder of realising Jesus was alive! As the sun rose and the birds began to sing, it seemed that Jesus Himself was very near to them as they worshipped together.

As everyone returned to the campsite, they were all ready for a hearty breakfast, including decorated eggs which the leaders had prepared.

Later a walk through the forest had been arranged for the group, and they set out in good spirits. It was a sort of nature treasure hunt, and each tent had a list of things to try and find or see. Tyler's tent had a great advantage because he was very skilled in tracking. He made the group of boys quieten down and told them they must be like Red Indians and track silently if they were to see wildlife. His advice paid off, for before too long they came across a herd of Sika deer. They were beautiful to watch, such elegant creatures. Later on they came to a mire, a boggy area. Here there were lots of mosses and liverwort and other bog plants. They saw some strange fungi too. Paul wished his sister was around to draw them!

The girls' tent which Flick was in became entranced by a large herd of New Forest ponies grazing on some heath land. It was hard to realise they were wild animals, they looked so docile and gentle. It took a while for them to look for other things, but eventually they did find lots of wild flowers. Once again, Flick wished Tess was there to draw them, but another girl in the group made a very good attempt. They also saw several butterflies which they were able to identify with the help of a chart and the tent officer.

The second boys' tent did a lot of birdwatching. They didn't see too many of the hundred resident species, but they were pleased with their list of thirty-four! They, too, came upon some Roe deer, but because they were quite a noisy group, the deer soon scattered!

The smallest group was the tent with only two girls and a leader. They concentrated on a pond, looking for frogspawn and newts. As the morning became warmer, so the reptiles became more active. One of the girls stood on a stone and had no idea that an adder had come out from underneath it to bask in the sun. Unfortunately, she so surprised and cornered the snake that it struck out at her . She was terrified! However, because she was wearing jeans and 'wellies', it could not find any flesh to deposit its venom, so she was not bitten.

"Help, a snake!" she screamed. "It's an adder—look, it's trying to bite me!" And she ran screaming to the tent leader.

It took the leader a while to calm both girls down and make sure the girl wasn't hurt. They decided to leave that area to look for other creatures and plants away from the pond. The leader told them that the adder had only struck because he was cornered. Adders are more afraid of people than people are of them and normally would slither away very quickly if they heard a noise. They did stop and thank God for taking care of them. It would have been a real race to Bournemouth Hospital had the girl been bitten!

Being out in the forest on that Sunday morning gave the young people time to chat to each other and their leaders. The leader of Seb's tent was a university student who was studying engineering in Bristol. Seb really liked him and thought he would like to talk to him about his dilemma of becoming a Christian.

"Can I talk to you about something?" Seb asked the young man.

"Of course. What's on your mind?" he answered. The rest of the group were being directed by Tyler, and so it was easy for them to fall a little behind and talk privately.

"Ever since Good Friday I have been feeling so bad about myself. I keep thinking about the person I am and all the wrong things I have done and that it was things like these that sent Jesus to the cross. I want Jesus to forgive me, but … well, I don't know how to say this. If I'm really honest, I like to organise everything, and that includes how I live my life!" Seb blurted out. "I guess I want to know Jesus, but I'm not sure I want Him to be in control of my life."

The young man was quiet for a moment, and Seb wondered if he had shocked him by what he had said.

Finally, he answered. "Seb, thanks for being so honest. So many people pretend and are not honest, and God appreciates our honesty. Of course, He knows what we feel anyway, but He likes us to face up to it and tell him the truth. I'm not sure how to answer you altogether, because I haven't been a Christian very long. However, I have always wanted to be an engineer, and I became a Christian at the time when I was applying to uni. Someone told me that I should now ask God what I was to do with my life, and I was bothered in case God had other plans for me. I went to see my pastor and asked his advice because my parents don't go to church and don't believe in God."

"What did he say?" asked Seb, really interested in the story.

"He told me first of all that God has a plan for my life and showed me the verse in Jeremiah chapter twenty-nine, verse eleven. Then he told me that when God created me even in my mum's womb, he had created me with certain gifts and wanted me to use these to serve Him. That was very reassuring! The pastor's advice to me was to pray about where I should go to uni and apply for the course for which I was best suited. God was well able to open or shut doors if I was willing for His plans. Then he told me to work as hard as I could and get the best exam results I could manage. That was my responsibility, he said!"

Now it was Seb's turn to be quiet while he thought things through.

"So if I like organising, that can be a gift from God?" he asked.

"Most definitely," answered the student. "And God needs people with gifts like that in His church. When God asks us to follow Jesus, it isn't to deprive us or take away things from our lives; it is to fulfil us and make us the person He planned us to be. We really can trust Him to take care of us!"

"Then I want to make my choice to become a follower of Jesus," Seb said in a definite voice. "I so want Him to forgive me and to be able to sleep properly again without feeling so guilty. But I still have another problem!"

"So what's that, Seb?" asked the leader.

"You know I am a twin. Flick and I have always done everything together. I'm not sure she will understand," he answered.

"Seb, this is a decision between you and God. He has to be number one, and you will have to trust Him to work it out between you and Flick. He made you a twin too, so He understands the special relationship!"

Then the student went on to say, "In a way, it was a bit like that for me. I had a girlfriend who I really liked very much. We had been very close since year nine at school and even planned on going to the same uni and getting a flat together. When I became a Christian, I knew she wouldn't understand and I knew it would mean a change in my lifestyle because lots of things I was doing were not pleasing to God. I had to decide that I would follow Jesus even if it meant losing my girlfriend. And I did lose her, because she didn't want to become a Christian, so our relationship ended. It hurt a lot, but the joy of belonging to Jesus was far more than the hurt."

"Thank you for telling me that. You have helped me so much," said Seb. "I now know what I should do, and that is to give my life to Jesus."

The rest of the group were just a little ahead of them and busy with their treasure hunt, so Seb and his young tent officer stopped for a few minutes, and Seb prayed and asked God for forgiveness for all the wrong things in his life and asked Jesus to be his Saviour and Lord.

"Hallelujah!" shouted the student. "What a wonderful thing to happen on Easter day! Now you know in a real way that Jesus is alive!"

They ran to join the others, and Theo looked at his brother and knew something wonderful had happened to him because he face was full of happiness!

The rest of Easter Sunday passed so quickly! They had a Live Wires meeting after dinner, then a great game of volleyball before supper. The campfire meeting was again a very special time. As the sun went down, they sang lots of songs, and lots of the group said how special the weekend had been for them. Right at the end, Seb had the courage to say that he had given his life to Jesus that afternoon. He was glad it was dark and no one could see how much he was blushing. He looked over at Flick who was the other side of the fire, and she smiled at him. At least she wasn't angry. He hadn't had time to tell her before the campfire.

For Easter Monday, a sports competition had been arranged. Some games were serious, like volleyball, but other games were silly and a bit like 'It's a knockout!' It was all huge fun and gave everyone a chance to win lots of points for their tent. Because the numbers of boys and girls in the tents differed, one of the leaders who was very clever at maths worked out all the scores and averaged them, so it was completely fair. The winners were the Woodlarks, the boys' tent with three boys. Everyone clapped them as they received the prize of a tin of chocolates called 'Celebrations'. They opened them at once and shared them with everyone!

In the afternoon, they had to pack up and drive home. It had been a wonderful weekend, and everyone gave many thanks to the leaders. They sang all the way home, the favourite song being the Romany round!

Although they were home once more, they knew they had the rest of the Easter holidays with many exciting things still to do!